MAIN LIBRARY
ALBANY PUBLIC LIBRARY
W9-AMP-953

MAIN LIBRARY
ALBANY PUBLIC LIBRARY

PELLUCIDAR

The Mahar spread her giant wings and sped away.

PELLUCIDAR

EDGAR RICE BURROUGHS

DOVER PUBLICATIONS, INC.
Mineola, New York

Bibliographical Note

This Dover edition, first published in 2002, is an unabridged republication of the work first published by Grosset & Dunlap in 1923, and republished (with *At the Earth's Core* and *Tanar of Pellucidar*) by Dover Publications, Inc., in 1963.

Library of Congress Cataloging-in-Publication Data

Burroughs, Edgar Rice, 1875-1950.
    Pellucidar / Edgar Rice Burroughs.
       p. cm.
    ISBN 0-486-42869-9 (pbk.)
     1. Earth–Core–Fiction. I. Title.

PS3503.U687 P45 2003
813'.52–dc21
                                       2002034981

Manufactured in the United States of America
Dover Publications, Inc., 31 East 2nd Street, Mineola, N.Y. 11501

CONTENTS

Face to face with the Titan.

PROLOG

SEVERAL years had elapsed since I had found the opportunity to do any big-game hunting; but at last I had my plans almost perfected for a return to my old stamping-grounds in northern Africa, where in other days I had had excellent sport in pursuit of the king of beasts.

The date of my departure had been set; I was to leave in two weeks. No schoolboy counting the lagging hours that must pass before the beginning of "long vacation" released him to the delirious joys of the summer camp could have been filled with greater impatience or keener anticipation.

And then came a letter that started me for Africa twelve days ahead of my schedule.

Often am I in receipt of letters from strangers who have found something in a story of mine to commend or to condemn. My interest in this department of my correspondence is ever fresh. I opened this particular letter with all the zest of pleasurable anticipation with which I had opened so many others. The postmark (Algiers) had aroused my interest and curiosity, especially at this time, since it was Algiers that was presently to witness the termination of my coming sea voyage in search of sport and adventure.

Before the reading of that letter was completed lions and lion-hunting had fled my thoughts, and I was in a state of excitement bordering upon frenzy.

It—well, read it yourself, and see if you, too, do not find food for frantic conjecture, for tantalizing doubts, and for a great hope.

Here it is:

DEAR SIR: I think that I have run across one of the most remarkable coincidences in modern literature. But let me start at the beginning:

I am, by profession, a wanderer upon the face of the earth. I have no trade—nor any other occupation.

My father bequeathed me a competency; some remoter ancestor—a lust to roam. I have combined the two and invested them carefully and without extravagance.

I became interested in your story, *At the Earth's Core,* not so much because of the probability of the tale as of a great and abiding wonder that people should be paid real money for writing such impossible trash. You will pardon my candor, but it is necessary that you understand my mental attitude toward this particular story—that you may credit that which follows.

Shortly thereafter I started for the Sahara in search of a rather rare species of antelope that is to be found only occasionally within a limited area at a certain season of the year. My chase led me far from the haunts of civilized man.

It was a fruitless search, however, in so far as antelope is concerned; but one night as I lay courting sleep at the edge of a little cluster of date-palms that surround an ancient well in the midst of the arid, shifting sands, I suddenly became conscious of a strange sound coming apparently from the earth beneath my head.

It was an intermittent ticking!

No reptile or insect with which I am familiar reproduces any such notes. I lay for an hour—listening intently.

At last my curiosity got the better of me. I arose, lighted my lamp and commenced to investigate.

My bedding lay upon a rug stretched directly upon the warm sand. The noise appeared to be coming from beneath the rug. I raised it, but found nothing—yet, at intervals, the sound continued.

I dug into the sand with the point of my hunting-knife. A few inches below the surface of the sand I encountered a solid substance that had the feel of wood beneath the sharp steel.

Excavating about it, I unearthed a small wooden box. From this receptacle issued the strange sound that I had heard.

How had it come here?

What did it contain?

In attempting to lift it from its burying place I discovered that it seemed to be held fast by means of a very small insulated cable running farther into the sand beneath it.

My first impulse was to drag the thing loose by main strength; but fortunately I thought better of this and fell to examining the box. I soon saw that it was covered by a hinged lid, which was held closed by a simple screw-hook and eye.

It took but a moment to loosen this and raise the cover, when, to my utter astonishment, I discovered an ordinary telegraph instrument clicking away within.

"What in the world," thought I, "is this thing doing here?"

That it was a French military instrument was my first guess; but really there didn't seem much likelihood that this was the correct explanation, when one took into account the loneliness and remoteness of the spot.

As I sat gazing at my remarkable find, which was ticking and clicking away there in the silence of the desert night, trying to convey some message which I was unable to interpret, my eyes fell upon a bit of paper lying in the bottom of the box beside the instrument. I picked it up and examined it. Upon it were written but two letters:

D. I.

They meant nothing to me then. I was baffled.

Once, in an interval of silence upon the part of the receiving instrument, I moved the sending-key up and down a few times. Instantly the receiving mechanism commenced to work frantically.

I tried to recall something of the Morse Code, with which I had played as a little boy—but time had obliterated it from my memory. I became almost frantic as I let my imagination run riot among the possibilities for which this clicking instrument might stand.

Some poor devil at the unknown other end might be in dire need of succor. The very franticness of the instrument's wild clashing betokened something of the kind.

And there sat I, powerless to interpret, and so powerless to help!

It was then that the inspiration came to me. In a flash there leaped to my mind the closing paragraphs of the story I had read in the club at Algiers:

Does the answer lie somewhere upon the bosom of the broad Sahara, at the ends of two tiny wires, hidden beneath a lost cairn?

The idea seemed preposterous. Experience and intelligence combined to assure me that there could be no slightest grain of truth or possibility in your wild tale—it was fiction pure and simple.

And yet where *were* the other ends of those wires?

What was this instrument—ticking away here in the great Sahara—but a travesty upon the possible!

Would I have believed in it had I not seen it with my own eyes?

And the initials—D. I.—upon the slip of paper! David's initials were these—David Innes.

I smiled at my imaginings. I ridiculed the assumption that there was an inner world and that these wires led downward through the earth's crust to the surface of Pellucidar. And yet——

Well, I sat there all night, listening to that tantalizing clicking, now and then moving the sending-key just to let the other end know that the instrument had been discovered. In the morning, after carefully returning the box to its hole and covering it over with sand, I called my servants about me, snatched a hurried breakfast, mounted my horse, and started upon a forced march for Algiers.

I arrived here today. In writing you this letter I feel that I am making a fool of myself.

There is no David Innes.

There is no Dian the Beautiful.

There is no world within a world.

Pellucidar is but a realm of your imagination—nothing more.

But——

The incident of the finding of that buried telegraph instrument upon the lonely Sahara is little short of uncanny, in view of your story of the adventures of David Innes.

I have called it one of the most remarkable coincidences in modern fiction. I called it literature before, but—again pardon my candor—your story is not.

And now—why am I writing you?

Heaven knows, unless it is that the persistent clicking of that unfathomable enigma out there in the vast silences of the Sahara has so wrought upon my nerves that reason refuses longer to function sanely.

I cannot hear it now, yet I know that far away to the south, all alone beneath the sands, it is still pounding out its vain, frantic appeal.

It is maddening!

It is your fault—I want you to release me from it.

Cable me at once, at my expense, that there was no basis of fact for your story, *At the Earth's Core.*

Very respectfully yours,

COGDON NESTOR,
—— and —— Club,
Algiers.

June 1st, ——.

Ten minutes after reading this letter I had cabled Mr. Nestor as follows:

STORY TRUE. AWAIT ME ALGIERS.

As fast as train and boat would carry me, I sped toward my destination. For all those dragging days my mind was a whirl of mad conjecture, of frantic hope, of numbing fear.

The finding of the telegraph-instrument practically assured me that David Innes had driven Perry's iron mole back through the earth's crust to the buried world of Pellucidar; but what adventures had befallen him since his return?

Had he found Dian the Beautiful, his half-savage mate, safe among his friends, or had Hooja the Sly One succeeded in his nefarious schemes to abduct her?

Did Abner Perry, the lovable old inventor and paleontologist, still live?

Had the federated tribes of Pellucidar succeeded in overthrowing the mighty Mahars, the dominant race of reptilian monsters, and their fierce, gorilla-like soldiery, the savage Sagoths?

I must admit that I was in a state bordering upon nervous prostration when I entered the —— and —— Club, in Algiers, and inquired for Mr. Nestor. A moment later I was ushered into his presence, to find myself clasping hands with the sort of chap that the world holds only too few of.

He was a tall, smooth-faced man of about thirty, clean-cut, straight, and strong, and weather-tanned to the hue of a desert Arab. I liked him immensely from the first, and I hope that after our three months together in the desert country—three months not entirely lacking in adventure—he found that a man may be a writer of "impossible trash" and yet have some redeeming qualities.

The day following my arrival at Algiers we left for the south, Nestor having made all arrangements in advance, guessing, as he naturally did, that I could be coming to Africa for but a single purpose—to hasten at once to the buried telegraph-instrument and wrest its secret from it.

In addition to our native servants, we took along an English telegraph-operator named Frank Downes. Nothing of interest enlivened our journey by rail and caravan till we came to the cluster of date-palms about the ancient well upon the rim of the Sahara.

It was the very spot at which I first had seen David Innes. If he had ever raised a cairn above the telegraph instrument no sign of it remained now. Had it not been for the chance that caused Cogden Nestor to throw down his sleeping rug directly over the hidden instrument, it might still be clicking there unheard—and this story still unwritten.

When we reached the spot and unearthed the little box the instrument was quiet, nor did repeated attempts upon the part of our telegrapher succeed in winning a response from the other end of the line. After several days of futile endeavor to raise Pellucidar, we had begun to despair. I was as positive that the other end of that little cable protruded through the surface of the inner world as I am that I sit here today in my study—when about midnight of the fourth day I was awakened by the sound of the instrument.

Leaping to my feet I grasped Downes roughly by the neck and dragged him out of his blankets. He didn't need to be told what caused my excitement, for the instant he was awake he, too, heard the long-hoped-for click, and with a whoop of delight pounced upon the instrument.

Nestor was on his feet almost as soon as I. The three of us huddled about that little box as if our lives depended upon the message it had for us.

Downes interrupted the clicking with his sending-key. The noise of the receiver stopped instantly.

"Ask who it is, Downes," I directed.

He did so, and while we awaited the Englishman's translation of the reply, I doubt if either Nestor or I breathed.

"He says he's David Innes," said Downes. "He wants to know who we are."

"Tell him," said I; "and that we want to know how he is—and all that has befallen him since I last saw him."

For two months I talked with David Innes almost every day, and as Downes translated, either Nestor or I took notes. From these, arranged in chronological order, I have set down the following account of the further adventures of David Innes at the earth's core, practically in his own words.

CHAPTER I

LOST ON PELLUCIDAR

THE Arabs, of whom I wrote you at the end of my last letter (Innes began), and whom I thought to be enemies intent only upon murdering me, proved to be exceedingly friendly—they were searching for the very band of marauders that had threatened my existence. The huge rhamphorhynchus-like reptile that I had brought back with me from the inner world—the ugly Mahar that Hooja the Sly One had substituted for my dear Dian at the moment of my departure—filled them with wonder and with awe.

Nor less so did the mighty subterranean prospector which had carried me to Pellucidar and back again, and which lay out in the desert about two miles from my camp.

With their help I managed to get the unwieldy tons of its great bulk into a vertical position—the nose deep in a hole we had dug in the sand and the rest of it supported by the trunks of date-palms cut for the purpose.

It was a mighty engineering job with only wild Arabs and their wilder mounts to do the work of an electric crane—but finally it was completed, and I was ready for departure.

For some time I hesitated to take the Mahar back with me. She had been docile and quiet ever since she had discovered herself virtually a prisoner aboard the "iron mole." It had been, of course, impossible for me to communicate with her since she had no auditory organs and I no knowledge of her fourth-dimension, sixth-sense method of communication.

Naturally I am kind-hearted, and so I found it beyond me to leave even this hateful and repulsive thing alone in a strange and hostile world. The result was that when I entered the iron mole I took her with me.

That she knew that we were about to return to Pellucidar was evident, for immediately her manner changed from that of habitual gloom that had pervaded her, to an almost human expression of contentment and delight.

Our trip through the earth's crust was but a repetition of my two former journeys between the inner and the outer worlds. This time, however, I imagine that we must have maintained a more nearly perpendicular course, for we accomplished the journey in a few minutes' less time than upon the occasion of my first journey through the five-hundred-mile crust. Just a trifle less than seventy-two hours after our departure into the sands of the Sahara, we broke through the surface of Pellucidar.

Fortune once again favored me by the slightest of margins, for when I opened the door in the prospector's outer jacket I saw that we had missed coming up through the bottom of an ocean by but a few hundred yards.

The aspect of the surrounding country was entirely unfamiliar to me—I had no conception of precisely where I was upon the one hundred and twenty-four million square miles of Pellucidar's vast land surface.

The perpetual midday sun poured down its torrid rays from zenith, as it had done since the beginning of Pellucidarian time —as it would continue to do to the end of it. Before me, across the wide sea, the weird, horizonless seascape folded gently upward to meet the sky until it lost itself to view in the azure depths of distance far above the level of my eyes.

How strange it looked! How vastly different from the flat and puny area of the circumscribed vision of the dweller upon the outer crust!

I was lost. Though I wandered ceaselessly throughout a lifetime, I might never discover the whereabouts of my former friends of this strange and savage world. Never again might I see dear old Perry, nor Ghak the Hairy One, nor Dacor the Strong One, nor that other infinitely precious one—my sweet and noble mate, Dian the Beautiful!

But even so I was glad to tread once more the surface of Pellucidar. Mysterious and terrible, grotesque and savage though she is in many of her aspects, I cannot but love her. Her very savagery appealed to me, for it is the savagery of unspoiled Nature.

The magnificence of her tropic beauties enthralled me. Her mighty land areas breathed unfettered freedom.

Her untracked oceans, whispering of virgin wonders unsullied by the eye of man, beckoned me out upon their restless bosoms.

Not for an instant did I regret the world of my nativity. I was in Pellucidar. I was *home*. And I was content.

As I stood dreaming beside the giant thing that had brought me safely through the earth's crust, my traveling companion, the hideous Mahar, emerged from the interior of the prospector and stood beside me. For a long time she remained motionless.

What thoughts were passing through the convolutions of her reptilian brain?

I do not know.

She was a member of the dominant race of Pellucidar. By a strange freak of evolution her kind had first developed the power of reason in that world of anomalies.

To her, creatures such as I were of a lower order. As Perry had discovered among the writings of her kind in the buried city of Phutra, it was still an open question among the Mahars as to whether man possessed means of intelligent communication or the power of reason.

Her kind believed that in the center of all-pervading solidity there was a single, vast, spherical cavity, which was Pellucidar. This cavity had been left there for the sole purpose of providing a place for the creation and propagation of the Mahar race. Everything within it had been put there for the uses of the Mahar.

I wondered what this particular Mahar might think now. I found pleasure in speculating upon just what the effect had been upon her of passing through the earth's crust, and coming out into a world that one of even less intelligence than the great Mahars could easily see was a different world from her own Pellucidar.

What had she thought of the outer world's tiny sun?

What had been the effect upon her of the moon and myriad stars of the clear African nights?

How had she explained them?

With what sensations of awe must she first have watched the sun moving slowly across the heavens to disappear at last beneath the western horizon, leaving in his wake that which the Mahar had never before witnessed—the darkness of night? For upon Pellucidar there is no night. The stationary sun hangs forever in the center of the Pellucidarian sky—directly overhead.

Then, too, she must have been impressed by the wondrous mechanism of the prospector which had bored its way from world to world and back again. And that it had been driven by a rational being must also have occurred to her.

Too, she had seen me conversing with other men upon the earth's surface. She had seen the arrival of the caravan of books and arms, and ammunition, and the balance of the heterogeneous collection which I had crammed into the cabin of the iron mole for transportation to Pellucidar.

She had seen all these evidences of a civilization and brain-power transcending in scientific achievement anything that her race had produced; nor once had she seen a creature of her own kind.

There could have been but a single deduction in the mind of the Mahar—there were other worlds than Pellucidar, and the *gilak* was a rational being.

Now the creature at my side was creeping slowly toward the near-by sea. At my hip hung a long-barreled six-shooter—somehow I had been unable to find the same sensation of security in the new-fangled automatics that had been perfected since my first departure from the outer world—and in my hand was a heavy express rifle.

I could have shot the Mahar with ease, for I knew intuitively that she was escaping—but I did not.

I felt that if she could return to her own kind with the story of her adventures, the position of the human race within Pellucidar would be advanced immensely at a single stride, for at once man would take his proper place in the considerations of the reptilia.

At the edge of the sea the creature paused and looked back at me. Then she slid sinuously into the surf.

For several minutes I saw no more of her as she luxuriated in the cool depths.

Then a hundred yards from shore she rose and there for another short while she floated upon the surface.

Finally she spread her giant wings, flapped them vigorously a score of times and rose above the blue sea. A single time she circled far aloft—and then straight as an arrow she sped away.

I watched her until the distant haze enveloped her and she had disappeared. I was alone.

My first concern was to discover where within Pellucidar I might be—and in what direction lay the land of the Sarians where Ghak the Hairy One ruled.

But how was I to guess in which direction lay Sari?

And if I set out to search—what then?

Could I find my way back to the prospector with its priceless freight of books, firearms, ammunition, scientific instruments, and still more books—its great library of reference works upon every conceivable branch of applied sciences?

And if I could not, of what value was all this vast storehouse of potential civilization and progress to be to the world of my adoption?

Upon the other hand, if I remained here alone with it, what could I accomplish single-handed?

Nothing.

But where there was no east, no west, no north, no south, no stars, no moon, and only a stationary midday sun, how was I to find my way back to this spot should ever I get out of sight of it?

I didn't know.

For a long time I stood buried in deep thought, when it occurred to me to try out one of the compasses I had brought and ascertain if it remained steadily fixed upon an unvarying pole. I reentered the prospector and fetched a compass without.

Moving a considerable distance from the prospector that the needle might not be influenced by its great bulk of iron and steel, I turned the delicate instrument about in every direction.

Always and steadily the needle remained rigidly fixed upon a point straight out to sea, apparently pointing toward a large island some ten or twenty miles distant. This then should be north.

I drew my note-book from my pocket and made a careful topographical sketch of the locality within the range of my vision. Due north lay the island, far out upon the shimmering sea.

The spot I had chosen for my observations was the top of a large, flat boulder which rose six or eight feet above the turf. This spot I called Greenwich. The boulder was the "Royal Observatory."

I had made a start! I cannot tell you what a sense of relief was imparted to me by the simple fact that there was at least one spot within Pellucidar with a familiar name and a place upon a map.

It was with almost childish joy that I made a little circle in my note-book and traced the word Greenwich beside it.

Now I felt I might start out upon my search with some assurance of finding my way back again to the prospector.

I decided that at first I would travel directly south in the hope that I might in that direction find some familiar landmark. It was as good a direction as any. This much at least might be said of it.

Among the many other things I had brought from the outer world were a number of pedometers. I slipped three of these into

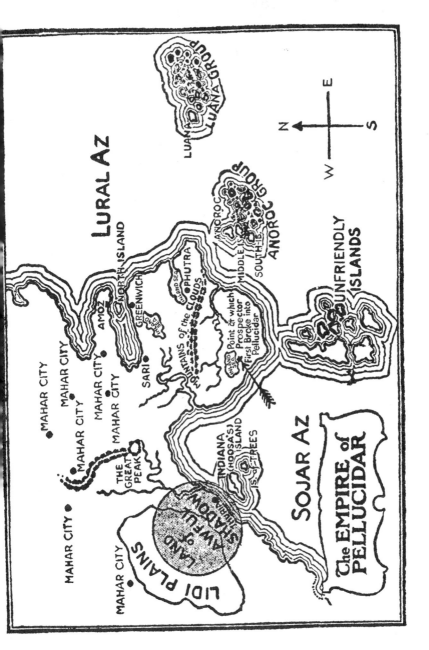

my pockets with the idea that I might arrive at a more or less accurate mean from the registrations of them all.

On my map I would register so many paces south, so many east, so many west, and so on. When I was ready to return I would then do so by any route that I might choose.

I also strapped a considerable quantity of ammunition across my shoulders, pocketed some matches, and hooked an aluminum fry-pan and a small stew-kettle of the same metal to my belt.

I was ready—ready to go forth and explore a world!

Ready to search a land area of 124,110,000 square miles for my friends, my incomparable mate, and good old Perry!

And so, after locking the door in the outer shell of the prospector, I set out upon my quest. Due south I traveled, across lovely valleys thick-dotted with grazing herds.

Through dense primeval forests I forced my way and up the slopes of mighty mountains searching for a pass to their farther sides.

Ibex and musk-sheep fell before my good old revolver, so that I lacked not for food in the higher altitudes. The forests and the plains gave plentifully of fruits and wild birds, antelope, aurochsen, and elk.

Occasionally, for the larger game animals and the gigantic beasts of prey, I used my express rifle, but for the most part the revolver filled all my needs.

There were times, too, when faced by a mighty cave bear, a saber-toothed tiger, or huge *felis spelaea*, black-maned and terrible, even my powerful rifle seemed pitifully inadequate—but fortune favored me so that I passed unscathed through adventures that even the recollection of causes the short hairs to bristle at the nape of my neck.

How long I wandered toward the south I do not know, for shortly after I left the prospector something went wrong with my watch, and I was again at the mercy of the baffling, timelessness of Pellucidar, forging steadily ahead beneath the great, motionless sun which hangs eternally at noon.

I ate many times, however, so that days must have elapsed, possibly months with no familiar landscape rewarding my eager eyes.

I saw no men nor signs of men. Nor is this strange, for Pellucidar, in its land area, is immense, while the human race there is very young and consequently far from numerous.

Doubtless upon that long search mine was the first human foot to touch the soil in many places—mine the first human eye to rest upon the gorgeous wonders of the landscape.

It was a staggering thought. I could not but dwell upon it often as I made my lonely way through this virgin world. Then, quite suddenly, one day I stepped out of the peace of manless primality into the presence of man—and peace was gone.

It happened thus:

I had been following a ravine downward out of a chain of lofty hills and had paused at its mouth to view the lovely little valley that lay before me. At one side was tangled wood, while straight ahead a river wound peacefully along parallel to the cliffs in which the hills terminated at the valley's edge.

Presently, as I stood enjoying the lovely scene, as insatiate for Nature's wonders as if I had not looked upon similar landscapes countless times, a sound of shouting broke from the direction of the woods. That the harsh, discordant notes rose from the throats of men I could not doubt.

I slipped behind a large boulder near the mouth of the ravine and waited. I could hear the crashing of underbrush in the forest, and I guessed that whoever came came quickly—pursued and pursuers, doubtless.

In a short time some hunted animal would break into view, and a moment later a score of half-naked savages would come leaping after with spears or clubs or great stone-knives.

I had seen the thing so many times during my life within Pellucidar that I felt that I could anticipate to a nicety precisely what I was about to witness. I hoped that the hunters would prove friendly and be able to direct me toward Sari.

Even as I was thinking these thoughts the quarry emerged from the forest. But it was no terrified four-footed beast. Instead, what I saw was an old man—a terrified old man!

Staggering feebly and hopelessly from what must have been some very terrible fate, if one could judge from the horrified expressions he continually cast behind him toward the wood, he came stumbling on in my direction.

He had covered but a short distance from the forest when I beheld the first of his pursuers—a Sagoth, one of those grim and terrible gorilla-men who guard the mighty Mahars in their buried cities, faring forth from time to time upon slave-raiding or punitive expeditions against the human race of Pellucidar, of whom the dominant race of the inner world think as we think of the bison or the wild sheep of our own world.

Close behind the foremost Sagoth came others until a full dozen raced, shouting after the terror-stricken old man. They would be upon him shortly, that was plain.

One of them was rapidly overhauling him, his back-thrown spear-arm testifying to his purpose.

And then, quite with the suddenness of an unexpected blow, I realized a past familiarity with the gait and carriage of the fugitive.

Simultaneously there swept over me the staggering fact that the old man was—*Perry!* That he was about to die before my very eyes with no hope that I could reach him in time to avert the awful catastrophe—for to me it meant a real catastrophe!

Perry was my best friend.

Dian, of course, I looked upon as more than friend. She was my mate—a part of me.

I had entirely forgotten the rifle in my hand and the revolvers at my belt; one does not readily synchronize his thoughts with the stone age and the twentieth century simultaneously.

Now from past habit I still thought in the stone age, and in my thoughts of the stone age there were no thoughts of firearms.

The fellow was almost upon Perry when the feel of the gun in my hand awoke me from the lethargy of terror that had gripped me. From behind my boulder I threw up the heavy express rifle —a mighty engine of destruction that might bring down a cave bear or a mammoth at a single shot—and let drive at the Sagoth's broad, hairy breast.

At the sound of the shot he stopped stockstill. His spear dropped from his hand.

Then he lunged forward upon his face.

The effect upon the others was little less remarkable. Perry alone could have possibly guessed the meaning of the loud report or explained its connection with the sudden collapse of the Sagoth. The other gorilla-men halted for but an instant. Then with renewed shrieks of rage they sprang forward to finish Perry.

At the same time I stepped from behind my boulder, drawing one of my revolvers that I might conserve the more precious ammunition of the express rifle. Quickly I fired again with the lesser weapon.

Then it was that all eyes were directed toward me. Another Sagoth fell to the bullet from the revolver; but it did not stop his companions. They were out for revenge as well as blood now, and they meant to have both.

As I ran forward toward Perry I fired four more shots, dropping three of our antagonists. Then at last the remaining seven wavered. It was too much for them, this roaring death that leaped, invisible, upon them from a great distance.

As they hesitated I reached Perry's side. I have never seen such an expression upon any man's face as that upon Perry's when he recognized me. I have no words wherewith to describe it. There was not time to talk then—scarce for a greeting. I thrust the full, loaded revolver into his hand, fired the last shot in my own, and reloaded. There were but six Sagoths left then.

They started toward us once more, though I could see that they were terrified probably as much by the noise of the guns as by their effects. They never reached us. Half-way the three that remained turned and fled, and we let them go.

The last we saw of them they were disappearing into the tangled undergrowth of the forest. And then Perry turned and threw his arms about my neck and, burying his old face upon my shoulder, wept like a child.

CHAPTER II

TRAVELING WITH TERROR

WE MADE camp there beside the peaceful river. There Perry told me all that had befallen him since I had departed for the outer crust.

It seemed that Hooja had made it appear that I had intentionally left Dian behind, and that I did not purpose ever returning to Pellucidar. He told them that I was of another world and that I had tired of this and of its inhabitants.

To Dian he had explained that I had a mate in the world to which I was returning; that I had never intended taking Dian the Beautiful back with me; and that she had seen the last of me.

Shortly afterward Dian had disappeared from the camp, nor had Perry seen or heard aught of her since.

He had no conception of the time that had elapsed since I had departed, but guessed that many years had dragged their slow way into the past.

Hooja, too, had disappeared very soon after Dian had left. The Sarians, under Ghak the Hairy One, and the Amozites under Dacor the Strong One, Dian's brother, had fallen out over my supposed defection, for Ghak would not believe that I had thus treacherously deceived and deserted them.

The result had been that these two powerful tribes had fallen upon one another with the new weapons that Perry and I had taught them to make and to use. Other tribes of the new federation took sides with the original disputants or set up petty revolutions of their own.

The result was the total demolition of the work we had so well started.

Taking advantage of the tribal war, the Mahars had gathered their Sagoths in force and fallen upon one tribe after another in rapid succession, wreaking awful havoc among them and reducing them for the most part to as pitiable a state of terror as that from which we had raised them.

Alone of all the once-mighty federation the Sarians and the Amozites with a few other tribes continued to maintain their defiance of the Mahars; but these tribes were still divided among themselves, nor had it seemed at all probable to Perry when he had last been among them that any attempt at re-amalgamation would be made.

"And thus, your majesty," he concluded, "has faded back into the oblivion of the Stone Age our wondrous dream and with it has gone the First Empire of Pellucidar."

We both had to smile at the use of my royal title, yet I was indeed still "Emperor of Pellucidar," and some day I meant to rebuild what the vile act of the treacherous Hooja had torn down.

But first I would find my empress. To me she was worth forty empires.

"Have you no clue as to the whereabouts of Dian?" I asked.

"None whatever," replied Perry. "It was in search of her that I came to the pretty pass in which you discovered me, and from which, David, you saved me.

"I knew perfectly well that you had not intentionally deserted either Dian or Pellucidar. I guessed that in some way Hooja the Sly One was at the bottom of the matter, and I determined to go to Amoz, where I guessed that Dian might come to the protection of her brother, and do my utmost to convince her, and through her Dacor the Strong One, that we had all been victims of a treacherous plot to which you were no party.

"I came to Amoz after a most trying and terrible journey, only to find that Dian was not among her brother's people and that they knew naught of her whereabouts.

"Dacor, I am sure, wanted to be fair and just, but so great were his grief and anger over the disappearance of his sister that he could not listen to reason, but kept repeating time and again that only your return to Pellucidar could prove the honesty of your intentions.

"Then came a stranger from another tribe, sent I am sure at the instigation of Hooja. He so turned the Amozites against me that I was forced to flee their country to escape assassination.

"In attempting to return to Sari I became lost, and then the Sagoths discovered me. For a long time I eluded them, hiding in caves and wading in rivers to throw them off my trail.

"I lived on nuts and fruits and the edible roots that chance threw in my way.

"I traveled on and on, in what directions I could not even guess; and at last I could elude them no longer and the end came as I had long foreseen that it would come, except that I had not foreseen that you would be there to save me."

We rested in our camp until Perry had regained sufficient strength to travel again. We planned much, rebuilding all our shattered air-castles; but above all we planned most to find Dian.

I could not believe that she was dead, yet where she might be in this savage world, and under what frightful conditions she might be living, I could not guess.

When Perry was rested we returned to the prospector, where he fitted himself out fully like a civilized human being—underclothing, socks, shoes, khaki jacket and breeches and good, substantial puttees.

When I had come upon him he was clothed in rough *sadok* sandals, a gee-string and a tunic fashioned from the shaggy hide of a *thag*. Now he wore real clothing again for the first time since the ape-folk had stripped us of our apparel that long-gone day that had witnessed our advent within Pellucidar.

With a bandoleer of cartridges across his shoulder, two six-shooters at his hips, and a rifle in his hand he was a much rejuvenated Perry.

Indeed he was quite a different person altogether from the rather shaky old man who had entered the prospector with me ten or eleven years before, for the trial trip that had plunged us into such wondrous adventures and into a strange and hitherto undreamed-of world.

Now he was straight and active. His muscles, almost atrophied from disuse in his former life, had filled out.

He was still an old man of course, but instead of appearing ten years older than he really was, as he had when we left the outer world, he now appeared about ten years younger. The wild, free life of Pellucidar had worked wonders for him.

Well, it must need have done so or killed him, for a man of Perry's former physical condition could not long have survived the dangers and rigors of the primitive life of the inner world.

Perry had been greatly interested in my map and in the "royal observatory" at Greenwich. By use of the pedometers we had retraced our way to the prospector with ease and accuracy.

Now that we were ready to set out again we decided to follow a different route on the chance that it might lead us into more familiar territory.

I shall not weary you with a repetition of the countless adventures of our long search. Encounters with wild beasts of gigantic size were of almost daily occurrence; but with our deadly express rifles we ran comparatively little risk when one recalls that previously we had both traversed this world of frightful dangers inadequately armed with crude, primitive weapons and all but naked.

We ate and slept many times—so many that we lost count—and so I do not know how long we roamed, though our map shows the distances and directions quite accurately. We must have covered a great many thousand square miles of territory, and yet we had seen nothing in the way of a familiar landmark, when from the heights of a mountain-range we were crossing I descried far in the distance great masses of billowing clouds.

Now clouds are practically unknown in the skies of Pellucidar. The moment that my eyes rested upon them my heart leaped. I seized Perry's arm and, pointing toward the horizonless distance, shouted:

"The Mountains of the Clouds!"

"They lie close to Phutra, and the country of our worst enemies, the Mahars," Perry remonstrated.

"I know it," I replied, "but they give us a starting-point from which to prosecute our search intelligently. They are at least a familiar landmark.

"They tell us that we are upon the right trail and not wandering far in the wrong direction.

"Furthermore, close to the Mountains of the Clouds dwells a good friend, Ja the Mezop. You did not know him, but you know all that he did for me and all that he will gladly do to aid me.

"At least he can direct us upon the right direction toward Sari."

"The Mountains of the Clouds constitute a mighty range," replied Perry. "They must cover an enormous territory. How are you to find your friend in all the great country that is visible from their rugged flanks?"

"Easily," I answered him, "for Ja gave me minute directions.
I recall almost his exact words:

" 'You need merely come to the foot of the highest peak of the
Mountains of the Clouds. There you will find a river that flows
into the Lural Az.

" 'Directly opposite the mouth of the river you will see three
large islands far out—so far that they are barely discernible. The
one to the extreme left as you face them from the mouth of the
river is Anoroc, where I rule the tribe of Anoroc.' "

And so we hastened onward toward the great cloud-mass that
was to be our guide for several weary marches. At last we came
close to the towering crags, Alp-like in their grandeur.

Rising nobly among its noble fellows, one stupendous peak
reared its giant head thousands of feet above the others. It was
he whom we sought; but at its foot no river wound down toward
any sea.

"It must rise from the opposite side," suggested Perry, casting
a rueful glance at the forbidding heights that barred our further
progress. "We cannot endure the arctic cold of those high flung
passes, and to traverse the endless miles about this interminable
range might require a year or more. The land we seek must lie
upon the opposite side of the mountains."

"Then we must cross them," I insisted.

Perry shrugged.

"We can't do it, David," he repeated. "We are dressed for the
tropics. We should freeze to death among the snows and glaciers
long before we had discovered a pass to the opposite side."

"We must cross them," I reiterated. "We will cross them."

I had a plan, and that plan we carried out. It took some time.

First we made a permanent camp part way up the slopes where
there was good water. Then we set out in search of the great,
shaggy cave bear of the higher altitudes.

He is a mighty animal—a terrible animal. He is but little larger
than his cousin of the lesser, lower hills; but he makes up for it in
the awfulness of his ferocity and in the length and thickness of his
shaggy coat. It was his coat that we were after.

We came upon him quite unexpectedly. I was trudging in advance along a rocky trail worn smooth by the padded feet of countless ages of wild beasts. At a shoulder of the mountain around
which the path ran I came face to face with the Titan.

I was going up for a fur coat. He was coming down for breakfast. Each realized that here was the very thing he sought.

With a horrid roar the beast charged me.

At my right the cliff rose straight upward for thousands of feet.

At my left it dropped into a dim, abysmal cañon.

In front of me was the bear.

Behind me was Perry.

I shouted to him in warning, and then I raised my rifle and fired into the broad breast of the creature. There was no time to take aim; the thing was too close upon me.

But that my bullet took effect was evident from the howl of rage and pain that broke from the frothing jowls. It didn't stop him, though.

I fired again, and then he was upon me. Down I went beneath his ton of maddened, clawing flesh and bone and sinew.

I thought my time had come. I remember feeling sorry for poor old Perry, left all alone in this inhospitable, savage world.

And then of a sudden I realized that the bear was gone and that I was quite unharmed. I leaped to my feet, my rifle still clutched in my hand, and looked about for my antagonist.

I thought that I should find him farther down the trail, probably finishing Perry, and so I leaped in the direction I supposed him to be, to find Perry perched upon a projecting rock several feet above the trail. My cry of warning had given him time to reach this point of safety.

There he squatted, his eyes wide and his mouth ajar, the picture of abject terror and consternation.

"Where is he?" he cried when he saw me. "Where is he?"

"Didn't he come this way?" I asked.

"Nothing came this way," replied the old man. "But I heard his roars—he must have been as large as an elephant."

"He was," I admitted; "but where in the world do you suppose he disappeared to?"

Then came a possible explanation to my mind. I returned to the point at which the bear had hurled me down and peered over the edge of the cliff into the abyss below.

Far, far down I saw a small brown blotch near the bottom of the cañon. It was the bear.

My second shot must have killed him, and so his dead body, after hurling me to the path, had toppled over into the abyss. I shivered at the thought of how close I, too, must have been to going over with him.

It took us a long time to reach the carcass, and arduous labor to remove the great pelt. But at last the thing was accomplished, and we returned to camp dragging the heavy trophy behind us.

Here we devoted another considerable period to scraping and

curing it. When this was done to our satisfaction we made heavy boots, trousers, and coats of the shaggy skin, turning the fur in.

From the scraps we fashioned caps that came down around our ears, with flaps that fell about our shoulders and breasts. We were now fairly well equipped for our search for a pass to the opposite side of the Mountains of the Clouds.

Our first step now was to move our camp upward to the very edge of the perpetual snows which cap this lofty range. Here we built a snug, secure little hut, which we provisioned and stored with fuel for its diminutive fireplace.

With our hut as a base we sallied forth in search of a pass across the range.

Our every move was carefully noted upon our maps which we now kept in duplicate. By this means we were saved tedious and unnecessary retracing of ways already explored.

Systematically we worked upward in both directions from our base, and when we had at last discovered what seemed might prove a feasible pass we moved our belongings to a new hut farther up.

It was hard work—cold, bitter, cruel work. Not a step did we take in advance but the grim reaper strode silently in our tracks.

There were the great cave bears in the timber, and gaunt, lean wolves—huge creatures twice the size of our Canadian timberwolves. Farther up we were assailed by enormous white bears—hungry, devilish fellows, who came roaring across the rough glacier tops at the first glimpse of us, or stalked us stealthily by scent when they had not yet seen us.

It is one of the peculiarities of life within Pellucidar that man is more often the hunted than the hunter. Myriad are the huge-bellied carnivora of this primitive world. Never, from birth to death, are those great bellies sufficiently filled, so always are their mighty owners prowling about in search of meat.

Terribly armed for battle as they are, man presents to them in his primal state an easy prey, slow of foot, puny of strength, ill-equipped by nature with natural weapons of defense.

The bears looked upon us as easy meat. Only our heavy rifles saved us from prompt extinction. Poor Perry never was a raging lion at heart, and I am convinced that the terrors of that awful period must have caused him poignant mental anguish.

When we were abroad pushing our trail farther and farther toward the distant break which, we assumed, marked a feasible way across the range, we never knew at what second some great engine of clawed and fanged destruction might rush upon us from behind, or lie in wait for us beyond an ice-hummock or a jutting shoulder of the craggy steeps.

The roar of our rifles was constantly shattering the world-old silence of stupendous cañons upon which the eye of man had never before gazed. And when in the comparative safety of our hut we lay down to sleep the great beasts roared and fought without the walls, clawed and battered at the door, or rushed their colossal frames headlong against the hut's sides until it rocked and trembled to the impact.

Yes, it was a gay life.

Perry had got to taking stock of our ammunition each time we returned to the hut. It became something of an obsession with him.

He'd count our cartridges one by one and then try to figure how long it would be before the last was expended and we must either remain in the hut until we starved to death or venture forth, empty, to fill the belly of some hungry bear.

I must admit that I, too, felt worried, for our progress was indeed snail-like, and our ammunition could not last forever. In discussing the problem, finally we came to the decision to burn our bridges behind us and make one last supreme effort to cross the divide.

It would mean that we must go without sleep for a long period, and with the further chance that when the time came that sleep could no longer be denied we might still be high in the frozen regions of perpetual snow and ice, where sleep would mean certain death, exposed as we would be to the attacks of wild beasts and without shelter from the hideous cold.

But we decided that we must take these chances, and so at last we set forth from our hut for the last time, carrying such necessities as we felt we could least afford to do without. The bears seemed unusually troublesome and determined that time, and as we clambered slowly upward beyond the highest point to which we had previously attained, the cold became infinitely more intense.

Presently, with two great bears dogging our footsteps we entered a dense fog.

We had reached the heights that are so often cloud-wrapped for long periods. We could see nothing a few paces beyond our noses.

We dared not turn back into the teeth of the bears which we could hear grunting behind us. To meet them in this bewildering fog would have been to court instant death.

Perry was almost overcome by the hopelessness of our situation. He flopped down on his knees and began to pray.

It was the first time I had heard him at his old habit since my return to Pellucidar, and I had thought that he had given up his little idiosyncrasy; but he hadn't. Far from it.

I let him pray for a short time undisturbed, and then as I was about to suggest that we had better be pushing along one of the bears in our rear let out a roar that made the earth fairly tremble beneath our feet.

It brought Perry to his feet as if he had been stung by a wasp, and sent him racing ahead through the blinding fog at a gait that I knew must soon end in disaster were it not checked.

Crevasses in the glacier-ice were far too frequent to permit of reckless speed even in a clear atmosphere, and then there were hideous precipices along the edges of which our way often led us. I shivered as I thought of the poor old fellow's peril.

At the top of my lungs I called to him to stop, but he did not answer me. And then I hurried on in the direction he had gone, faster by far than safety dictated.

For a while I thought I heard him ahead of me, but at last, though I paused often to listen and to call to him, I heard nothing more, not even the grunting of the bears that had been behind us. All was deathly silence—the silence of the tomb. About me lay the thick, impenetrable fog.

I was alone. Perry was gone—gone forever, I had not the slightest doubt.

Somewhere near by lay the mouth of a treacherous fissure, and far down at its icy bottom lay all that was mortal of my old friend, Abner Perry. There would his body lie preserved in its icy sepulcher for countless ages, until on some far distant day the slow-moving river of ice had wound its snail-like way down to the warmer level, there to disgorge its grisly evidence of grim tragedy, and what, in that far future age, might mean baffling mystery.

CHAPTER III

SHOOTING THE CHUTES—AND AFTER

THROUGH the fog I felt my way along by means of my compass. I no longer heard the bears, nor did I encounter one within the fog.

Experience has since taught me that these great beasts are as terror-stricken by this phenomenon as a landsman by a fog at sea, and that no sooner does a fog envelop them than they make the best of their way to lower levels and a clear atmosphere. It was well for me that this was true.

I felt very sad and lonely as I crawled along the difficult footing. My own predicament weighed less heavily upon me than the loss of Perry, for I loved the old fellow.

That I should ever win the opposite slopes of the range I began to doubt, for though I am naturally sanguine, I imagine that the bereavement which had befallen me had cast such a gloom over my spirits that I could see no slightest ray of hope for the future.

Then, too, the blighting, gray oblivion of the cold, damp clouds through which I wandered was depressing. Hope thrives best in sunlight, and I am sure that it does not thrive at all in a fog.

But the instinct of self-preservation is stronger than hope. It thrives, fortunately, upon nothing. It takes root upon the brink of the grave, and blossoms in the jaws of death. Now it flourished bravely upon the breast of dead hope, and urged me onward and upward in a stern endeavor to justify its existence.

As I advanced the fog became denser. I could see nothing beyond my nose. Even the snow and ice I trod were invisible.

I could not see below the breast of my bearskin coat. I seemed to be floating in a sea of vapor.

To go forward over a dangerous glacier under such conditions was little short of madness; but I could not have stopped going had I known positively that death lay two paces before my nose. In the first place, it was too cold to stop, and in the second, I should have gone mad but for the excitement of the perils that beset each forward step.

For some time the ground had been rougher and steeper, until I had been forced to scale a considerable height that had carried me from the glacier entirely. I was sure from my compass that I was following the right general direction, and so I kept on.

Once more the ground was level. From the wind that blew about me I guessed that I must be upon some exposed peak or ridge.

And then quite suddenly I stepped out into space. Wildly I turned and clutched at the ground that had slipped from beneath my feet.

Only a smooth, icy surface was there. I found nothing to clutch or stay my fall, and a moment later so great was my speed that nothing could have stayed me.

As suddenly as I had pitched into space, with equal suddenness did I emerge from the fog, out of which I shot like a projectile from a cannon into clear daylight. My speed was so great that I could see nothing about me but a blurred and indistinct sheet of smooth and frozen snow, that rushed past me with express-train velocity.

I must have slid downward thousands of feet before the steep incline curved gently on to a broad, smooth, snow-covered plateau. Across this I hurtled with slowly diminishing velocity, until at last objects about me began to take definite shape.

Far ahead, miles and miles away, I saw a great valley and mighty woods, and beyond these a broad expanse of water. In the nearer foreground I discerned a small, dark blob of color upon the shimmering whiteness of the snow.

"A bear," thought I, and thanked the instinct that had impelled me to cling tenaciously to my rifle during the moments of my awful tumble.

At the rate I was going it would be but a moment before I should be quite abreast the thing; nor was it long before I came to a sudden stop in soft snow, upon which the sun was shining, not twenty paces from the object of my most immediate apprehension.

It was standing upon its hind legs waiting for me. As I scrambled to my feet to meet it, I dropped my gun in the snow and doubled up with laughter.

It was Perry.

The expression upon his face, combined with the relief I felt at seeing him again safe and sound, was too much for my overwrought nerves.

"David!" he cried. "David, my boy! God has been good to an old man. He has answered my prayer."

It seems that Perry in his mad flight had plunged over the brink at about the same point as that at which I had stepped over it a short time later. Chance had done for us what long periods of rational labor had failed to accomplish.

We had crossed the divide. We were upon the side of the Mountains of the Clouds that we had for so long been attempting to reach.

We looked about. Below us were green trees and warm jungles. In the distance was a great sea.

"The Lural Az," I said, pointing toward its blue-green surface.

Somehow—the gods alone can explain it—Perry, too, had clung to his rifle during his mad descent of the icy slope. For that there was cause for great rejoicing.

Neither of us was worse for his experience, so after shaking the snow from our clothing, we set off at a great rate down toward the warmth and comfort of the forest and the jungle.

The going was easy by comparison with the awful obstacles we had had to encounter upon the opposite side of the divide. There were beasts, of course, but we came through safely.

Before we halted to eat or rest, we stood beside a little mountain brook beneath the wondrous trees of the primeval forest in an atmosphere of warmth and comfort. It reminded me of an early June day in the Maine woods.

We fell to work with our short axes and cut enough small trees to build a rude protection from the fiercer beasts. Then we lay down to sleep.

How long we slept I do not know. Perry says that inasmuch as there is no means of measuring time within Pellucidar, there can be no such thing as time here, and that we may have slept an outer earthly year, or we may have slept but a second.

But this I know. We had stuck the ends of some of the saplings into the ground in the building of our shelter, first stripping the leaves and branches from them, and when we awoke we found that many of them had thrust forth sprouts.

Personally, I think that we slept at least a month; but who may say? The sun marked midday when we closed our eyes; it was still in the same position when we opened them; nor had it varied a hair's breadth in the interim.

It is most baffling, this question of elapsed time within Pellucidar.

Anyhow, I was famished when we awoke. I think that it was the pangs of hunger that awoke me. Ptarmigan and wild boar fell before my revolver within a dozen moments of my awakening. Perry soon had a roaring fire blazing by the brink of the little stream.

It was a good and delicious meal we made. Though we did not eat the entire boar, we made a very large hole in him, while the ptarmigan was but a mouthful.

Having satisfied our hunger, we determined to set forth at once in search of Anoroc and my old friend, Ja the Mezop. We each thought that by following the little stream downward, we should come upon the large river which Ja had told me emptied into the Lural Az opposite his island.

We did so; nor were we disappointed, for at last after a pleasant journey—and what journey would not be pleasant after the hardships we had endured among the peaks of the Mountains of the Clouds—we came upon a broad flood that rushed majestically onward in the direction of the great sea we had seen from the snowy slopes of the mountains.

For three long marches we followed the left bank of the growing river, until at last we saw it roll its mighty volume into the vast waters of the sea. Far out across the rippling ocean we descried three islands. The one to the left must be Anoroc.

At last we had come close to a solution of our problem—the road to Sari.

But how to reach the islands was now the foremost question in our minds. We must build a canoe.

Perry is a most resourceful man. He has an axiom which carries the thought-kernel that what man has done, man can do, and it doesn't cut any figure with Perry whether a fellow knows how to do it or not.

He set out to make gunpowder once, shortly after our escape from Phutra and at the beginning of the confederation of the wild tribes of Pellucidar. He said that some one, without any knowledge of the fact that such a thing might be concocted, had once stumbled upon it by accident, and so he couldn't see why a fellow who knew all about powder except how to make it couldn't do as well.

He worked mighty hard mixing all sorts of things together, until finally he evolved a substance that looked like powder. He had been very proud of the stuff, and had gone about the village of the Sarians exhibiting it to every one who would listen to him, and explaining what its purpose was and what terrific havoc it would work, until finally the natives became so terrified at the stuff that they wouldn't come within a rod of Perry and his invention.

Finally, I suggested that we experiment with it and see what it would do, so Perry built a fire, after placing the powder at a safe distance, and then touched a glowing ember to a minute particle of the deadly explosive. It extinguished the ember.

Repeated experiments with it determined me that in searching for a high explosive, Perry had stumbled upon a fire-extinguisher that would have made his fortune for him back in our own world.

So now he set himself to work to build a scientific canoe. I had suggested that we construct a dugout, but Perry convinced me that we must build something more in keeping with our positions of supermen in this world of the Stone Age.

"We must impress these natives with our superiority," he explained. "You must not forget, David, that you are emperor of Pellucidar. As such you may not with dignity approach the shores of a foreign power in so crude a vessel as a dugout."

I pointed out to Perry that it wasn't much more incongruous for the emperor to cruise in a canoe, than it was for the prime minister to attempt to build one with his own hands.

He had to smile at that; but in extenuation of his act he assured me that it was quite customary for prime ministers to give their personal attention to the building of imperial navies; "and this," he said, "is the imperial navy of his Serene Highness, David I, Emperor of the Federated Kingdoms of Pellucidar."

I grinned; but Perry was quite serious about it. It had always seemed rather more or less of a joke to me that I should be addressed as majesty and all the rest of it. Yet my imperial power and dignity had been a very real thing during my brief reign.

Twenty tribes had joined the federation, and their chiefs had sworn eternal fealty to one another and to me. Among them were many powerful though savage nations. Their chiefs we had made kings; their tribal lands kingdoms.

We had armed them with bows and arrows and swords, in addition to their own more primitive weapons. I had trained them in military discipline and in so much of the art of war as I had gleaned from extensive reading of the campaigns of Napoleon, Von Moltke, Grant, and the ancients.

We had marked out as best we could natural boundaries dividing the various kingdoms. We had warned tribes beyond these boundaries that they must not trespass, and we had marched against and severely punished those who had.

We had met and defeated the Mahars and the Sagoths. In short, we had demonstrated our rights to empire, and very rapidly were we being recognized and heralded abroad when my departure for the outer world and Hooja's treachery had set us back.

But now I had returned. The work that fate had undone must be done again, and though I must need smile at my imperial honors, I none the less felt the weight of duty and obligation that rested upon my shoulders.

Slowly the imperial navy progressed toward completion. She was a wondrous craft, but I had my doubts about her. When I voiced them to Perry, he reminded me gently that my people for many generations had been mine-owners, not ship-builders, and consequently I couldn't be expected to know much about the matter.

I was minded to inquire into his hereditary fitness to design battleships; but inasmuch as I already knew that his father had been a minister in a backwoods village far from the coast, I hesitated lest I offend the dear old fellow.

He was immensely serious about his work, and I must admit that in so far as appearances went he did extremely well with the meager tools and assistance at his command. We had only two short axes and our hunting-knives; yet with these we hewed trees, split them into planks, surfaced and fitted them.

The "navy" was some forty feet in length by ten feet beam. Her sides were quite straight and fully ten feet high—"for the purpose," explained Perry, "of adding dignity to her appearance and rendering it less easy for an enemy to board her."

As a matter of fact, I knew that he had had in mind the safety of her crew under javelin-fire—the lofty sides made an admirable shelter. Inside she reminded me of nothing so much as a floating trench. There was also some slight analogy to a huge coffin.

Her prow sloped sharply backward from the water-line—quite like a line of battle-ship. Perry had designed her more for her moral effect upon an enemy, I think, than for any real harm she might inflict, and so those parts which were to show were the most imposing.

Below the water-line she was practically non-existent. She should have had considerable draft; but, as the enemy couldn't have seen it, Perry decided to do away with it, and so made her flat-bottomed. It was this that caused my doubts about her.

There was another little idiosyncrasy of design that escaped us both until she was about ready to launch—there was no method of propulsion. Her sides were far too high to permit the use of sweeps, and when Perry suggested that we pole her, I remonstrated on the grounds that it would be a most undignified and awkward manner of sweeping down upon the foe, even if we could find or wield poles that would reach to the bottom of the ocean.

Finally I suggested that we convert her into a sailing vessel. When once the idea took hold Perry was most enthusiastic about it, and nothing would do but a four-masted, full-rigged ship.

Again I tried to dissuade him, but he was simply crazy over the psychological effect which the appearance of this strange and mighty craft would have upon the natives of Pellucidar. So we rigged her with thin hides for sails and dried gut for rope.

Neither of us knew much about sailing a full-rigged ship; but that didn't worry me a great deal, for I was confident that we should never be called upon to do so, and as the day of launching approached I was positive of it.

We had built her upon a low bank of the river close to where it emptied into the sea, and just above high tide. Her keel we had laid upon several rollers cut from small trees, the ends of the rollers in turn resting upon parallel tracks of long saplings. Her stern was toward the water.

A few hours before we were ready to launch her she made quite an imposing picture, for Perry had insisted upon setting every shred of "canvas." I told him that I didn't know much about it, but I was sure that at launching the hull only should have been completed, everything else being completed after she had floated safely.

At the last minute there was some delay while we sought a name for her. I wanted her christened the Perry in honor both of her designer and that other great naval genius of another world, Captain Oliver Hazard Perry, of the United States Navy. But Perry was too modest; he wouldn't hear of it.

We finally decided to establish a system in the naming of the fleet. Battle-ships of the first class should bear the names of kingdoms of the federation; armored cruisers the names of kings; cruisers the names of cities, and so on down the line. Therefore, we decided to name the first battle-ship *Sari*, after the first of the federated kingdoms.

The launching of the *Sari* proved easier than I contemplated. Perry wanted me to get in and break something over the bow as she floated out upon the bosom of the river, but I told him that I should feel safer on dry land until I saw which side up the *Sari* would float.

I could see by the expression of the old man's face that my words had hurt him; but I noticed that he didn't offer to get in himself, and so I felt less contrition than I might otherwise.

When we cut the ropes and removed the blocks that held the *Sari* in place she started for the water with a lunge. Before she hit it she was going at a reckless speed, for we had laid our tracks quite down to the water, greased them, and at intervals placed rollers all ready to receive the ship as she moved forward with stately dignity. But there was no dignity in the *Sari*.

When she touched the surface of the river she must have been going twenty or thirty miles an hour. Her momentum carried her well out into the stream, until she came to a sudden halt at the end of the long line which we had had the foresight to attach to her bow and fasten to a large tree upon the bank.

The moment her progress was checked she promptly capsized. Perry was overwhelmed. I didn't upbraid him, nor remind him that I had "told him so."

His grief was so genuine and so apparent that I didn't have the heart to reproach him, even were I inclined to that particular sort of meanness.

"Come, come, old man!" I cried. "It's not as bad as it looks. Give me a hand with this rope, and we'll drag her up as far as we can; and then when the tide goes out we'll try another scheme. I think we can make a go of her yet."

Well, we managed to get her up into shallow water. When the tide receded she lay there on her side in the mud, quite a pitiable object for the premier battle-ship of a world—"the terror of the seas" was the way Perry had occasionally described her.

We had to work fast; but before the tide came in again we had stripped her of her sails and masts, righted her, and filled her about a quarter full of rock ballast. If she didn't stick too fast in the mud I was sure that she would float this time right side up.

I can tell you that it was with palpitating hearts that we sat upon the river-bank and watched that tide come slowly in. The tides of Pellucidar don't amount to much by comparison with our higher tides of the outer world, but I knew that it ought to prove ample to float the *Sari*.

Nor was I mistaken. Finally we had the satisfaction of seeing the vessel rise out of the mud and float slowly up-stream with the tide. As the water rose we pulled her in quite close to the bank and clambered aboard.

She rested safely now upon an even keel; nor did she leak, for she was well calked with fiber and tarry pitch. We rigged up a single short mast and light sail, fastened planking down over the ballast to form a deck, worked her out into midstream with a couple of sweeps, and dropped our primitive stone anchor to await the turn of the tide that would bear us out to sea.

While we waited we devoted the time to the construction of an upper deck, since the one immediately above the ballast was some seven feet from the gunwale. The second deck was four feet above this. In it was a large, commodious hatch, leading to the lower deck. The sides of the ship rose three feet above the upper deck, forming an excellent breastwork, which we loopholed at intervals that we might lie prone and fire upon an enemy.

Though we were sailing out upon a peaceful mission in search of my friend Ja, we knew that we might meet with people of some other island who would prove unfriendly.

At last the tide turned. We weighed anchor. Slowly we drifted down the great river toward the sea.

About us swarmed the mighty denizens of the primeval deep—plesiosauri and ichthyosauri with all their horrid, slimy cousins whose names were as the names of aunts and uncles to Perry, but which I have never been able to recall an hour after having heard them.

At last we were safely launched upon the journey to which we had looked forward for so long, and the results of which meant so much to me.

CHAPTER IV

FRIENDSHIP AND TREACHERY

THE *Sari* proved a most erratic craft. She might have done well enough upon a park lagoon if safely anchored, but upon the bosom of a mighty ocean she left much to be desired.

Sailing with the wind she did her best; but in quartering or when close-hauled she drifted terribly, as a nautical man might have guessed she would. We couldn't keep within miles of our course, and our progress was pitifully slow.

Instead of making for the island of Anoroc, we bore far to the right, until it became evident that we should have to pass between the two right-hand islands and attempt to return toward Anoroc from the opposite side.

As we neared the islands Perry was quite overcome by their beauty. When we were directly between two of them he fairly went into raptures; nor could I blame him.

The tropical luxuriance of the foliage that dipped almost to the water's edge and the vivid colors of the blooms that shot the green made a most gorgeous spectacle.

Perry was right in the midst of a flowery panegyric on the wonders of the peaceful beauty of the scene when a canoe shot out from the nearest island. There were a dozen warriors in it; it was quickly followed by a second and third.

Of course we couldn't know the intentions of the strangers, but we could pretty well guess them.

Perry wanted to man the sweeps and try to get away from them, but I soon convinced him that any speed of which the *Sari* was capable would be far too slow to outdistance the swift, though awkward, dugouts of the Mezops.

I waited until they were quite close enough to hear me, and then I hailed them. I told them that we were friends of the Mezops, and that we were upon a visit to Ja of Anoroc, to which they replied that they were at war with Ja, and that if we would wait a minute they'd board us and throw our corpses to the azdyryths.

I warned them that they would get the worst of it if they didn't leave us alone, but they only shouted in derision and paddled swiftly toward us. It was evident that they were considerably impressed by the appearance and dimensions of our craft, but as these fellows know no fear they were not at all awed.

Seeing that they were determined to give battle, I leaned over the rail of the *Sari* and brought the imperial battle-squadron of the Emperor of Pellucidar into action for the first time in the history of a world. In other and simpler words, I fired my revolver at the nearest canoe.

The effect was magical. A warrior rose from his knees, threw his paddle aloft, stiffened into rigidity for an instant, and then toppled overboard.

The others ceased paddling, and, with wide eyes, looked first at me and then at the battling sea-things which fought for the corpse of their comrade. To them it must have seemed a miracle that I should be able to stand at thrice the range of the most powerful javelin-thrower and with a loud noise and a smudge of smoke slay one of their number with an invisible missile.

But only for an instant were they paralyzed with wonder. Then, with savage shouts, they fell once more to their paddles and forged rapidly toward us.

Again and again I fired. At each shot a warrior sank to the bottom of the canoe or tumbled overboard.

When the prow of the first craft touched the side of the *Sari* it contained only dead and dying men. The other two dugouts were approaching rapidly, so I turned my attention toward them.

I think that they must have been commencing to have some doubts—those wild, naked, red warriors—for when the first man fell in the second boat the others stopped paddling and commenced to jabber among themselves.

The third boat pulled up alongside the second and its crew joined in the conference. Taking advantage of the lull in the battle, I called out to the survivors to return to their shore.

"I have no fight with you," I cried, and then I told them who I was and added that if they would live in peace they must sooner or later join forces with me.

"Go back now to your people," I counseled them, "and tell them that you have seen David I, Emperor of the Federated Kingdoms of Pellucidar, and that single-handed he has overcome you, just as he intends overcoming the Mahars and the Sagoths and any other peoples of Pellucidar who threaten the peace and welfare of his empire."

Slowly they turned the noses of their canoes toward land. It was evident that they were impressed; yet that they were loath to give up without further contesting my claim to naval supremacy was also apparent, for some of their number seemed to be exhorting the others to a renewal of the conflict.

However, at last they drew slowly away, and the *Sari,* which had not decreased her snail-like speed during this, her first engagement, continued upon her slow, uneven way.

Presently Perry stuck his head up through the hatch and hailed me.

"Have the scoundrels departed?" he asked. "Have you killed them all?"

"Those whom I failed to kill have departed, Perry," I replied.

He came out on deck and, peering over the side, descried the lone canoe floating a short distance astern with its grim and grisly freight. Farther his eyes wandered to the retreating boats.

"David," said he at last, "this is a notable occasion. It is a great day in the annals of Pellucidar. We have won a glorious victory.

"Your majesty's navy has routed a fleet of the enemy thrice its own size, manned by ten times as many men. Let us give thanks."

I could scarce restrain a smile at Perry's use of the pronoun "we," yet I was glad to share the rejoicing with him as I shall always be glad to share everything with the dear old fellow.

Perry is the only male coward I have ever known whom I could respect and love. He was not created for fighting; but I think that if the occasion should ever arise where it became necessary he would give his life cheerfully for me—yes, I *know* it.

It took us a long time to work around the islands and draw in close to Anoroc. In the leisure afforded we took turns working on our map, and by means of the compass and a little guesswork we set down the shoreline we had left and the three islands with fair accuracy.

Crossed sabers marked the spot where the first great naval engagement of a world had taken place. In a note-book we jotted down, as had been our custom, details that would be of historical value later.

Opposite Anoroc we came to anchor quite close to shore. I knew from my previous experience with the tortuous trails of the island that I could never find my way inland to the hidden tree-village of the Mezop chieftain, Ja; so we remained aboard the *Sari*, firing our express rifles at intervals to attract the attention of the natives.

After some ten shots had been fired at considerable intervals a body of copper-colored warriors appeared upon the shore. They watched us for a moment and then I hailed them, asking the whereabouts of my old friend Ja.

They did not reply at once, but stood with their heads together in serious and animated discussion. Continually they turned their eyes toward our strange craft. It was evident that they were greatly puzzled by our appearance as well as unable to explain the source of the loud noises that had attracted their attention to us. At last one of the warriors addressed us.

"Who are you who seek Ja?" he asked. "What would you of our chief?"

"We are friends," I replied. "I am David. Tell Ja that David, whose life he once saved from a *sithic,* has come again to visit him.

"If you will send out a canoe we will come ashore. We cannot bring our great warship closer in."

Again they talked for a considerable time. Then two of them entered a canoe that several dragged from its hiding-place in the jungle and paddled swiftly toward us.

They were magnificent specimens of manhood. Perry had never seen a member of this red race close to before. In fact, the dead men in the canoe we had left astern after the battle and the survivors who were paddling rapidly toward their shore were the first he ever had seen. He had been greatly impressed by their physical beauty and the promise of superior intelligence which their well-shaped skulls gave.

The two who now paddled out received us into their canoe with dignified courtesy. To my inquiries relative to Ja they explained that he had not been in the village when our signals were heard, but that runners had been sent out after him and that doubtless he was already upon his way to the coast.

One of the men remembered me from the occasion of my former visit to the island; he was extremely agreeable the moment that he came close enough to recognize me. He said that Ja would be delighted to welcome me, and that all the tribe of Anoroc knew of me by repute, and had received explicit instructions from their chieftain that if any of them should ever come upon me to show me every kindness and attention.

Upon shore we were received with equal honor. While we stood conversing with our bronze friends a tall warrior leaped suddenly from the jungle.

It was Ja. As his eyes fell upon me his face lighted with pleasure. He came quickly forward to greet me after the manner of his tribe.

Toward Perry he was equally hospitable. The old man fell in love with the savage giant as completely as had I. Ja conducted us along the maze-like trail to his strange village, where he gave over one of the tree-houses for our exclusive use.

Perry was much interested in the unique habitation, which resembled nothing so much as a huge wasp's nest built around the bole of a tree well above the ground.

After we had eaten and rested Ja came to see us with a number of his head men. They listened attentively to my story, which included a narrative of the events leading to the formation of the federated kingdoms, the battle with the Mahars, my journey to the outer world, and my return to Pellucidar and search for Sari and my mate.

Ja told me that the Mezops had heard something of the federation and had been much interested in it. He had even gone so far as to send a party of warriors toward Sari to investigate the reports, and to arrange for the entrance of Anoroc into the empire in case it appeared that there was any truth in the rumors that one of the aims of the federation was the overthrow of the Mahars.

The delegation had met with a party of Sagoths. As there had been a truce between the Mahars and the Mezops for many generations, they camped with these warriors of the reptiles, from whom they learned that the federation had gone to pieces. So the party returned to Anoroc.

When I showed Ja our map and explained its purpose to him, he was much interested. The location of Anoroc, the Mountains of the Clouds, the river, and the strip of seacoast were all familiar to him.

He quickly indicated the position of the inland sea and, close beside it, the city of Phutra, where one of the powerful Mahar nations had its seat. He likewise showed us where Sari should be and carried his own coast-line as far north and south as it was known to him.

His additions to the map convinced us that Greenwich lay upon the verge of this same sea, and that it might be reached by water more easily than by the arduous crossing of the mountains or the dangerous approach through Phutra, which lay almost directly in line between Anoroc and Greenwich to the northwest.

If Sari lay upon the same water then the shore-line must bend far back toward the southwest of Greenwich—an assumption which, by the way, we found later to be true. Also, Sari was upon a lofty plateau at the southern end of a mighty gulf of the Great Ocean.

The location which Ja gave to distant Amoz puzzled us, for it placed it due north of Greenwich, apparently in mid-ocean. As Ja had never been so far and knew only of Amoz through hearsay, we thought that he must be mistaken; but he was not. Amoz lies directly north of Greenwich across the mouth of the same gulf as that upon which Sari is.

The sense of direction and location of these primitive Pellucidarians is little short of uncanny, as I have had occasion to remark in the past. You may take one of them to the uttermost ends of his world, to places of which he has never even heard, yet without sun or moon or stars to guide him, without map or compass, he will travel straight for home in the shortest direction.

Mountains, rivers, and seas may have to be gone around, but never once does his sense of direction fail him—the homing instinct is supreme.

In the same remarkable way they never forget the location of any place to which they have ever been, and know that of many of which they have only heard from others who have visited them.

In short, each Pellucidarian is a walking geography of his own district and of much of the country contiguous thereto. It always proved of the greatest aid to Perry and me; nevertheless we were anxious to enlarge our map, for we at least were not endowed with the homing instinct.

After several long councils it was decided that, in order to expedite matters, Perry should return to the prospector with a strong party of Mezops and fetch the freight I had brought from the outer world. Ja and his warriors were much impressed by our firearms, and were also anxious to build boats with sails.

As we had arms at the prospector and also books on boat-building we thought that it might prove an excellent idea to start these naturally maritime people upon the construction of a well built navy of stanch sailing-vessels. I was sure that with definite plans to go by Perry could oversee the construction of an adequate flotilla.

I warned him, however, not to be too ambitious, and to forget about dreadnoughts and armored cruisers for a while and build instead a few small sailing-boats that could be manned by four or five men.

I was to proceed to Sari, and while prosecuting my search for Dian attempt at the same time the rehabilitation of the federation. Perry was going as far as possible by water, with the chances that the entire trip might be made in that manner, which proved to be the fact.

With a couple of Mezops as companions I started for Sari. In order to avoid crossing the principal range of the Mountains of the Clouds we took a route that passed a little way south of Phutra. We had eaten four times and slept once, and were, as my companions told me, not far from the great Mahar city, when we were suddenly confronted by a considerable band of Sagoths.

They did not attack us, owing to the peace which exists between the Mahars and the Mezops, but I could see that they looked upon me with considerable suspicion. My friends told them that I was a stranger from a remote country, and as we had previously planned against such a contingency I pretended ignorance of the language which the human beings of Pellucidar employ in conversing with the gorilla-like soldiery of the Mahars.

I noticed, and not without misgivings, that the leader of the Sagoths eyed me with an expression that betokened partial recognition. I was sure that he had seen me before during the period of my incarceration in Phutra and that he was trying to recall my identity.

It worried me not a little. I was extremely thankful when we bade them adieu and continued upon our journey.

Several times during the next few marches I became acutely conscious of the sensation of being watched by unseen eyes, but I did not speak of my suspicions to my companions. Later I had reason to regret my reticence, for——

Well, this is how it happened:

We had killed an antelope and after eating our fill I had lain down to sleep. The Pellucidarians, who seem seldom if ever to require sleep, joined me in this instance, for we had had a very trying march along the northern foothills of the Mountains of the Clouds, and now with their bellies filled with meat they seemed ready for slumber.

When I awoke it was with a start to find a couple of huge Sagoths astride me. They pinioned my arms and legs, and later chained my wrists behind my back. Then they let me up.

I saw my companions; the brave fellows lay dead where they had slept, javelined to death without a chance at self-defense.

I was furious. I threatened the Sagoth leader with all sorts of dire reprisals; but when he heard me speak the hybrid language that is the medium of communication between his kind and the human race of the inner world he only grinned, as much as to say, "I thought so!"

They had not taken my revolvers or ammunition away from me because they did not know what they were; but my heavy rifle I had lost. They simply left it where it had lain beside me.

So low in the scale of intelligence are they, that they had not sufficient interest in this strange object even to fetch it along with them.

I knew from the direction of our march that they were taking me to Phutra. Once there I did not need much of an imagination to picture what my fate would be. It was the arena and a wild thag or fierce tarag for me—unless the Mahars elected to take me to the pits.

In that case my end would be no more certain, though infinitely more horrible and painful, for in the pits I should be subjected to cruel vivisection. From what I had once seen of their methods in the pits of Phutra I knew them to be the opposite of merciful, whereas in the arena I should be quickly despatched by some savage beast.

Arrived at the underground city, I was taken immediately before a slimy Mahar. When the creature had received the report of the Sagoth its cold eyes glistened with malice and hatred as they were turned balefully upon me.

I knew then that my identity had been guessed. With a show of excitement that I had never before seen evinced by a member of the dominant race of Pellucidar, the Mahar hustled me away, heavily guarded, through the main avenue of the city to one of the principal buildings.

Here we were ushered into a great hall where presently many Mahars gathered.

In utter silence they conversed, for they have no oral speech since they are without auditory nerves. Their method of communication Perry has likened to the projection of a sixth sense into a fourth dimension, where it becomes cognizable to the sixth sense of their audience.

Be that as it may, however, it was evident that I was the subject of discussion, and from the hateful looks bestowed upon me not a particularly pleasant subject.

How long I waited for their decision I do not know, but it must have been a very long time. Finally one of the Sagoths addressed me. He was acting as interpreter for his masters.

"The Mahars will spare your life," he said, "and release you on one condition."

"And what is that condition?" I asked, though I could guess its terms.

"That you return to them that which you stole from the pits of Phutra when you killed the four Mahars and escaped," he replied.

I had thought that that would be it. The great secret upon which depended the continuance of the Mahar race was safely hid where only Dian and I knew.

I ventured to imagine that they would have given me much more than my liberty to have it safely in their keeping again; but after that—what?

Would they keep their promises?

I doubted it. With the secret of artificial propagation once more in their hands their numbers would soon be made so to overrun the world of Pellucidar that there could be no hope for the eventual supremacy of the human race, the cause for which I so devoutly hoped, for which I had consecrated my life, and for which I was now willing to give my life.

Yes! In that moment as I stood before the heartless tribunal I felt that my life would be a very little thing to give could it save to the human race of Pellucidar the chance to come into its own by insuring the eventual extinction of the hated, powerful Mahars.

"Come!" exclaimed the Sagoths. "The mighty Mahars await your reply."

"You may say to them," I answered, "that I shall not tell them where the great secret is hid."

When this had been translated to them there was a great beating of reptilian wings, gaping of sharp-fanged jaws, and hideous hissing. I thought that they were about to fall upon me on the spot, and so I laid my hands upon my revolvers; but at length they became more quiet and presently transmitted some command to my Sagoth guard, the chief of which laid a heavy hand upon my arm and pushed me roughly before him from the audience-chamber.

They took me to the pits, where I lay carefully guarded. I was sure that I was to be taken to the vivisection laboratory, and it required all my courage to fortify myself against the terrors of so fearful a death. In Pellucidar, where there is no time, death-agonies may endure for eternities.

Accordingly, I had to steel myself against an endless doom, which now stared me in the face!

CHAPTER V

SURPRISES

BUT at last the allotted moment arrived—the moment for which I had been trying to prepare myself, for how long I could not even guess. A great Sagoth came and spoke some words of command to those who watched over me. I was jerked roughly to my feet and with little consideration hustled upward toward the higher levels.

Out into the broad avenue they conducted me, where, amid huge throngs of Mahars, Sagoths, and heavily guarded slaves, I was led, or, rather, pushed and shoved roughly, along in the same direction that the mob moved. I had seen such a concourse of people once before in the buried city of Phutra; I guessed, and rightly, that we were bound for the great arena where slaves who are condemned to death meet their end.

Into the vast amphitheater they took me, stationing me at the extreme end of the arena. The queen came, with her slimy, sickening retinue. The seats were filled. The show was about to commence.

Then, from a little doorway in the opposite end of the structure, a girl was led into the arena. She was at a considerable distance from me. I could not see her features.

I wondered what fate awaited this other poor victim and myself, and why they had chosen to have us die together. My own fate, or rather, my thought of it, was submerged in the natural pity I felt for this lone girl, doomed to die horribly beneath the cold, cruel eyes of her awful captors. Of what crime could she be guilty that she must expiate it in the dreaded arena?

As I stood thus thinking, another door, this time at one of the long sides of the arena, was thrown open, and into the theater of death slunk a mighty tarag, the huge cave tiger of the Stone Age. At my sides were my revolvers. My captors had not taken them from me, because they did not yet realize their nature. Doubtless they thought them some strange manner of war-club, and as those who are condemned to the arena are permitted weapons of defense, they let me keep them.

The girl they had armed with a javelin. A brass pin would have been almost as effective against the ferocious monster they had loosed upon her.

The tarag stood for a moment looking about him—first up at the vast audience and then about the arena. He did not seem to see me at all, but his eyes fell presently upon the girl. A hideous roar broke from his titanic lungs—a roar which ended in a long-drawn scream that is more human than the death-cry of a tortured woman—more human but more awesome. I could scarce restrain a shudder.

Slowly the beast turned and moved toward the girl. Then it was that I came to myself and to a realization of my duty. Quickly and as noiselessly as possible I ran down the arena in pursuit of the grim creature. As I ran I drew one of my pitifully futile weapons. Ah! Could I but have had my lost express-gun in my hands at that moment! A single well-placed shot would have crumpled even this great monster. The best I could hope to accomplish was to divert the thing from the girl to myself and then to place as many bullets as possible in it before it reached and mauled me into insensibility and death.

There is a certain unwritten law of the arena that vouchsafes freedom and immunity to the victor, be he beast or human being—both of whom, by the way, are all the same to the Mahar. That is, they were accustomed to look upon man as a lower animal before Perry and I broke through the Pellucidarian crust, but I imagine that they were beginning to alter their views a trifle and to realize that in the *gilak*—their word for human being—they had a highly organized, reasoning being to contend with.

Be that as it may, the chances were that the tarag alone would profit by the law of the arena. A few more of his long strides, a prodigious leap, and he would be upon the girl. I raised a revolver and fired. The bullet struck him in the left hind leg. It couldn't have damaged him much; but the report of the shot brought him around, facing me.

I think the snarling visage of a huge, enraged, saber-toothed tiger is one of the most terrible sights in the world. Especially if he be snarling at you and there be nothing between the two of you but bare sand.

Even as he faced me a little cry from the girl carried my eyes beyond the brute to her face. Hers was fastened upon me with an expression of incredulity that baffles description. There was both hope and horror in them, too.

"Dian!" I cried. "My Heavens, Dian!"

I saw her lips form the name David, as with raised javelin she rushed forward upon the tarag. She was a tigress then—a primitive savage female defending her loved one. Before she could reach the beast with her puny weapon, I fired again at the point where the tarag's neck met his left shoulder. If I could get a bullet through there it might reach his heart. The bullet didn't reach his heart, but it stopped him for an instant.

It was then that a strange thing happened. I heard a great hissing from the stands occupied by the Mahars, and as I glanced toward them I saw three mighty *thipdars*—the winged dragons that guard the queen, or, as Perry calls them, pterodactyls—rise swiftly from their rocks and dart lightning-like, toward the center of the arena. They are huge, powerful reptiles. One of them, with the advantage which his wings might give him, would easily be a match for a cave bear or a tarag.

These three, to my consternation, swooped down upon the tarag as he was gathering himself for a final charge upon me. They buried their talons in his back and lifted him bodily from the arena as if he had been a chicken in the clutches of a hawk.

What could it mean?

I was baffled for an explanation; but with the tarag gone I lost no time in hastening to Dian's side. With a little cry of delight she threw herself into my arms. So lost were we in the ecstasy of reunion that neither of us—to this day—can tell what became of the tarag.

The first thing we were aware of was the presence of a body of Sagoths about us. Gruffly they commanded us to follow them. They led us from the arena and back through the streets of Phutra to the audience chamber in which I had been tried and sentenced. Here we found ourselves facing the same cold, cruel tribunal.

Again a Sagoth acted as interpreter. He explained that our lives had been spared because at the last moment Tu-al-sa had returned to Phutra, and seeing me in the arena had prevailed upon the queen to spare my life.

"Who is Tu-al-sa?" I asked.

"A Mahar whose last male ancestor was—ages ago—the last of the male rulers among the Mahars," he replied.

"Why should she wish to have my life spared?"

He shrugged his shoulders and then repeated my question to

the Mahar spokesman. When the latter had explained in the strange sign-language that passes for speech between the Mahars and their fighting men the Sagoth turned again to me:

"For a long time you had Tu-al-sa in your power," he explained. "You might easily have killed her or abandoned her in a strange world—but you did neither. You did not harm her, and you brought her back with you to Pellucidar and set her free to return to Phutra. This is your reward."

Now I understood. The Mahar who had been my involuntary companion upon my return to the outer world was Tu-al-sa. This was the first time that I had learned the lady's name. I thanked fate that I had not left her upon the sands of the Sahara—or put a bullet in her, as I had been tempted to do. I was surprised to discover that gratitude was a characteristic of the dominant race of Pellucidar. I could never think of them as aught but cold-blooded, brainless reptiles, though Perry had devoted much time in explaining to me that owing to a strange freak of evolution among all the genera of the inner world, this species of the reptilia had advanced to a position quite analogous to that which man holds upon the outer crust.

He had often told me that there was every reason to believe from their writings, which he had learned to read while we were incarcerated in Phutra, that they were a just race, and that in certain branches of science and arts they were quite well advanced, especially in genetics and metaphysics, engineering and architecture.

While it had always been difficult for me to look upon these things as other than slimy, winged crocodiles—which, by the way, they do not at all resemble—I was now forced to a realization of the fact that I was in the hands of enlightened creatures—for justice and gratitude are certain hallmarks of rationality and culture.

But what they purposed for us further was of most imminent interest to me. They might save us from the tarag and yet not free us. They looked upon us yet, to some extent, I knew, as creatures of a lower order, and so as we are unable to place ourselves in the position of the brutes we enslave—thinking that they are happier in bondage than in the free fulfilment of the purposes for which nature intended them—the Mahars, too, might consider our welfare better conserved in captivity than among the dangers of the savage freedom we craved. Naturally, I was next impelled to inquire their further intent.

To my question, put through the Sagoth interpreter, I received the reply that having spared my life they considered that Tu-al-sa's debt of gratitude was canceled. They still had against me, however, the crime of which I had been guilty—the unforgivable crime of stealing the great secret. They, therefore, intended holding Dian and me prisoners until the manuscript was returned to them.

They would, they said, send an escort of Sagoths with me to fetch the precious document from its hiding-place, keeping Dian at Phutra as a hostage and releasing us both the moment that the document was safely restored to their queen.

There was no doubt but that they had the upper hand. However, there was so much more at stake than the liberty or even the lives of Dian and myself, that I did not deem it expedient to accept their offer without giving the matter careful thought.

Without the great secret this maleless race must eventually become extinct. For ages they had fertilized their eggs by an artificial process, the secret of which lay hidden in the little cave of a far-off valley where Dian and I had spent our honeymoon. I was none too sure that I could find the valley again, nor that I cared to. So long as the powerful reptilian race of Pellucidar continued to propagate, just so long would the position of man within the inner world be jeopardized. There could not be two dominant races.

I said as much to Dian.

"You used to tell me," she replied, "of the wonderful things you could accomplish with the inventions of your own world. Now you have returned with all that is necessary to place this great power in the hands of the men of Pellucidar.

"You told me of great engines of destruction which would cast a bursting ball of metal among our enemies, killing hundreds of them at one time.

"You told me of mighty fortresses of stone which a thousand men armed with big and little engines such as these could hold forever against a million Sagoths.

"You told me of great canoes which moved across the water without paddles, and which spat death from holes in their sides.

"All these may now belong to the men of Pellucidar. Why should we fear the Mahars?

"Let them breed! Let their numbers increase by thousands. They will be helpless before the power of the Emperor of Pellucidar.

"But if you remain a prisoner in Phutra, what may we accomplish?

"What could the men of Pellucidar do without you to lead them?

"They would fight among themselves, and while they fought the

Mahars would fall upon them, and even though the Mahar race should die out, of what value would the emancipation of the human race be to them without the knowledge, which you alone may wield, to guide them toward the wonderful civilization of which you have told me so much that I long for its comforts and luxuries as I never before longed for anything.

"No, David; the Mahars cannot harm us if you are at liberty. Let them have their secret that you and I may return to our people, and lead them to the conquest of all Pellucidar."

It was plain that Dian was ambitious, and that her ambition had not dulled her reasoning faculties. She was right. Nothing could be gained by remaining bottled up in Phutra for the rest of our lives.

It was true that Perry might do much with the contents of the prospector, or iron mole, in which I had brought down the implements of outer-world civilization; but Perry was a man of peace. He could never weld the warring factions of the disrupted federation. He could never win new tribes to the empire. He would fiddle around manufacturing gunpowder and trying to improve upon it until some one blew him up with his own invention. He wasn't practical. He never would get anywhere without a balance-wheel—without some one to direct his energies.

Perry needed me and I needed him. If we were going to do anything for Pellucidar we must be free to do it together.

The outcome of it all was that I agreed to the Mahars' proposition. They promised that Dian would be well treated and protected from every indignity during my absence. So I set out with a hundred Sagoths in search of the little valley which I had stumbled upon by accident, and which I might and might not find again.

We traveled directly toward Sari. Stopping at the camp where I had been captured I recovered my express rifle, for which I was very thankful. I found it lying where I had left it when I had been overpowered in my sleep by the Sagoths who had captured me and slain my Mezop companions.

On the way I added materially to my map, an occupation which did not elicit from the Sagoths even a shadow of interest. I felt that the human race of Pellucidar had little to fear from these gorilla-men. They were fighters—that was all. We might even use them later ourselves in this same capacity. They had not sufficient brain power to constitute a menace to the advancement of the human race.

As we neared the spot where I hoped to find the little valley I became more and more confident of success. Every landmark was familiar to me, and I was sure now that I knew the exact location of the cave.

It was at about this time that I sighted a number of the half-naked warriors of the human race of Pellucidar. They were marching across our front. At sight of us they halted; that there would be a fight I could not doubt. These Sagoths would never permit an opportunity for the capture of slaves for their Mahar masters to escape them.

I saw that the men were armed with bows and arrows, long lances and swords, so I guessed that they must have been members of the federation, for only my people had been thus equipped. Before Perry and I came the men of Pellucidar had only the crudest weapons wherewith to slay one another.

The Sagoths, too, were evidently expecting battle. With savage shouts they rushed forward toward the human warriors.

Then a strange thing happened. The leader of the human beings stepped forward with upraised hands. The Sagoths ceased their war-cries and advanced slowly to meet him. There was a long parley during which I could see that I was often the subject of their discourse. The Sagoths' leader pointed in the direction in which I had told him the valley lay. Evidently he was explaining the nature of our expedition to the leader of the warriors. It was all a puzzle to me.

What human being could be upon such excellent terms with the gorilla-men?

I couldn't imagine. I tried to get a good look at the fellow, but the Sagoths had left me in the rear with a guard when they had advanced to battle, and the distance was too great for me to recognize the features of any of the human beings.

Finally the parley was concluded and the men continued on their way while the Sagoths returned to where I stood with my guard. It was time for eating, so we stopped where we were and made our meal. The Sagoths didn't tell me who it was they had met, and I did not ask, though I must confess that I was quite curious.

They permitted me to sleep at this halt. Afterward we took up the last leg of our journey. I found the valley without difficulty and led my guard directly to the cave. At its mouth the Sagoths halted and I entered alone.

I noticed as I felt about the floor in the dim light that there was a pile of fresh-turned rubble there. Presently my hands came to the spot where the great secret had been buried. There was a cavity where I had carefully smoothed the earth over the hiding-place of the document—the manuscript was gone!

Frantically I searched the whole interior of the cave several times over, but without other result than a complete confirmation of my worst fears. Someone had been here ahead of me and stolen the great secret.

The one thing within Pellucidar which might free Dian and me was gone, nor was it likely that I should ever learn its whereabouts. If a Mahar had found it, which was quite improbable, the chances were that the dominant race would never divulge the fact that they had recovered the precious document. If a cave man had happened upon it he would have no conception of its meaning or value, and as a consequence it would be lost or destroyed in short order.

With bowed head and broken hopes I came out of the cave and told the Sagoth chieftain what I had discovered. It didn't mean much to the fellow, who doubtless had but little better idea of the contents of the document I had been sent to fetch to his masters than would the cave man who in all probability had discovered it.

The Sagoth knew only that I had failed in my mission, so he took advantage of the fact to make the return journey to Phutra as disagreeable as possible. I did not rebel, though I had with me the means to destroy them all. I did not dare rebel because of the consequences to Dian. I intended demanding her release on the grounds that she was in no way guilty of the theft, and that my failure to recover the document had not lessened the value of the good faith I had had in offering to do so. The Mahars might keep me in slavery if they chose, but Dian should be returned safely to her people.

I was full of my scheme when we entered Phutra and I was conducted directly to the great audience-chamber. The Mahars listened to the report of the Sagoth chieftain, and so difficult is it to judge their emotions from their almost expressionless countenances, that I was at a loss to know how terrible might be their wrath as they learned that their great secret, upon which rested the fate of their race, might now be irretrievably lost.

Presently I could see that she who presided was communicating something to the Sagoth interpreter—doubtless something to be transmitted to me which might give me a forewarning of the fate which lay in store for me. One thing I had decided definitely: If they would not free Dian I should turn loose upon Phutra with my little arsenal. Alone I might even win to freedom, and if I could learn where Dian was imprisoned it would be worth the attempt to free her. My thoughts were interrupted by the interpreter.

"The mighty Mahars," he said, "are unable to reconcile your statement that the document is lost with your action in sending it to them by a special messenger. They wish to know if you have so soon forgotten the truth or if you are merely ignoring it."

"I sent them no document," I cried. "Ask them what they mean."

"They say," he went on after conversing with the Mahar for a moment, "that just before you returned to Phutra, Hooja the Sly One came, bringing the great secret with him. He said that you had sent him ahead with it, asking him to deliver it and return to Sari where you would await him, bringing the girl with him."

"Dian?" I gasped. "The Mahars have given over Dian into the keeping of Hooja?"

"Surely," he replied. "What of it? She is only a gilak," as you or I would say, "She is only a cow."

CHAPTER VI

A PENDENT WORLD

THE Mahars set me free as they had promised, but with strict injunctions never to approach Phutra or any other Mahar city. They also made it perfectly plain that they considered me a dangerous creature, and that having wiped the slate clean in so far as they were under obligations to me, they now considered me fair prey. Should I again fall into their hands, they intimated it would go ill with me.

They would not tell me in which direction Hooja had set forth with Dian, so I departed from Phutra, filled with bitterness against the Mahars, and rage toward the Sly One who had once again robbed me of my greatest treasure.

At first I was minded to go directly back to Anoroc; but upon second thought turned my face toward Sari, as I felt that somewhere in that direction Hooja would travel, his own country lying in that general direction.

Of my journey to Sari it is only necessary to say that it was fraught with the usual excitement and adventure, incident to all travel across the face of savage Pellucidar. The dangers, however, were greatly reduced through the medium of my armament. I often wondered how it had happened that I had ever survived the first ten years of my life within the inner world, when, naked and primitively armed, I had traversed great areas of her beast-ridden surface.

With the aid of my map, which I had kept with great care during my march with the Sagoths in search of the great secret, I arrived at Sari at last. As I topped the lofty plateau in whose rocky cliffs the principal tribe of Sarians find their cave-homes, a great hue and cry arose from those who first discovered me.

Like wasps from their nests the hairy warriors poured from their caves. The bows with their poison-tipped arrows, which I had taught them to fashion and to use, were raised against me. Swords of hammered iron—another of my innovations—menaced me, as with lusty shouts the horde charged down.

It was a critical moment. Before I should be recognized I might be dead. It was evident that all semblance of intertribal relationship had ceased with my going, and that my people had reverted to their former savage, suspicious hatred of all strangers. My garb must have puzzled them, too, for never before of course had they seen a man clothed in khaki and puttees.

Leaning my express rifle against my body I raised both hands aloft. It was the peace-sign that is recognized everywhere upon the surface of Pellucidar. The charging warriors paused and surveyed me. I looked for my friend Ghak, the Hairy One, king of Sari, and presently I saw him coming from a distance. Ah, but it was good to see his mighty, hairy form once more! A friend was Ghak—a friend well worth the having; and it had been some time since I had seen a friend.

Shouldering his way through the throng of warriors, the mighty chieftain advanced toward me. There was an expression of puzzlement upon his fine features. He crossed the space between the warriors and myself, halting before me.

I did not speak. I did not even smile. I wanted to see if Ghak, my principal lieutenant, would recognize me. For some time he stood there looking me over carefully. His eyes took in my large pith helmet, my khaki jacket, and bandoleers of cartridges, the two revolvers swinging at my hips, the large rifle resting against my body. Still I stood with my hands above my head. He examined my puttees and my strong tan shoes—a little the worse for wear now. Then he glanced up once more to my face. As his gaze rested there quite steadily for some moments I saw recognition tinged with awe creep across his countenance.

Presently without a word he took one of my hands in his and dropping to one knee raised my fingers to his lips. Perry had taught them this trick, nor ever did the most polished courtier of all the grand courts of Europe perform the little act of homage with greater grace and dignity.

Quickly I raised Ghak to his feet, clasping both his hands in mine. I think there must have been tears in my eyes then—I know I felt too full for words. The king of Sari turned toward his warriors.

"Our emperor has come back," he announced. "Come hither and——"

But he got no further, for the shouts that broke from those savage throats would have drowned the voice of heaven itself. I had never guessed how much they thought of me. As they clustered around, almost fighting for the chance to kiss my hand, I saw again the vision of empire which I had thought faded forever.

With such as these I could conquer a world. With such as these I *would* conquer one! If the Sarians had remained loyal, so too would the Amozites be loyal still, and the Kalians, and the Suvians, and all the great tribes who had formed the federation that was to emancipate the human race of Pellucidar.

Perry was safe with the Mezops; I was safe with the Sarians; now if Dian were but safe with me the future would look bright indeed.

It did not take long to outline to Ghak all that had befallen me since I had departed from Pellucidar, and to get down to the business of finding Dian, which to me at that moment was of even greater importance than the very empire itself.

When I told him that Hooja had stolen her, he stamped his foot in rage.

"It is always the Sly One!" he cried. "It was Hooja who caused the first trouble between you and the Beautiful One.

"It was Hooja who betrayed our trust, and all but caused our recapture by the Sagoths that time we escaped from Phutra.

"It was Hooja who tricked you and substituted a Mahar for Dian when you started upon your return journey to your own world.

"It was Hooja who schemed and lied until he had turned the kingdoms one against another and destroyed the federation.

"When we had him in our power we were foolish to let him live. Next time——"

Ghak did not need to finish his sentence.

"He has become a very powerful enemy now," I replied. "That he is allied in some way with the Mahars is evidenced by the familiarity of his relations with the Sagoths who were accompanying me in search of the great secret, for it must have been Hooja whom I saw conversing with them just before we reached the valley. Doubtless they told him of our quest and he hastened on ahead of us, discovered the cave and stole the document. Well does he deserve his appellation of the Sly One."

With Ghak and his head men I held a number of consultations. The upshot of them was a decision to combine our search for Dian with an attempt to rebuild the crumbled federation. To this end twenty warriors were despatched in pairs to ten of the leading kingdoms, with instructions to make every effort to discover the whereabouts of Hooja and Dian, while prosecuting their missions to the chieftains to whom they were sent.

Ghak was to remain at home to receive the various delegations which we invited to come to Sari on the business of the federation. Four hundred warriors were started for Anoroc to fetch Perry and the contents of the prospector, to the capital of the empire, which was also the principal settlement of the Sarians.

At first it was intended that I remain at Sari, that I might be in readiness to hasten forth at the first report of the discovery of Dian; but I found the inaction in the face of my deep solicitude for the welfare of my mate so galling that scarce had the several units departed upon their missions before I, too, chafed to be actively engaged upon the search.

It was after my second sleep, subsequent to the departure of the warriors, as I recall, that I at last went to Ghak with the admission that I could no longer support the intolerable longing to be personally upon the trail of my lost love.

Ghak tried to dissuade me, though I could tell that his heart was with me in my wish to be away and really doing something. It was while we were arguing upon the subject that a stranger, with hands above his head, entered the village. He was immediately surrounded by warriors and conducted to Ghak's presence.

The fellow was a typical cave man—squat, muscular, and hairy, and of a type I had not seen before. His features, like those of all the primeval men of Pellucidar, were regular and fine. His weapons consisted of a stone ax and knife and a heavy knobbed bludgeon of wood. His skin was very white.

"Who are you?" asked Ghak. "And whence come you?"

"I am Kolk, son of Goork, who is chief of the Thurians," replied the stranger. "From Thuria I have come in search of the land of Amoz, where dwells Dacor, the Strong One, who stole my sister, Canda, the Graceful One, to be his mate.

"We of Thuria have heard of a great chieftain who has bound together many tribes, and my father has sent me to Dacor to learn if there be truth in these stories, and if so to offer the services of Thuria to him whom we have heard called emperor."

"The stories are true," replied Ghak, "and here is the emperor of whom you have heard. You need travel no farther."

Kolk was delighted. He told us much of the wonderful resources of Thuria, the Land of Awful Shadow, and of his long journey in search of Amoz.

"And why," I asked, "does Goork, your father, desire to join his kingdom to the empire?"

"There are two reasons," replied the young man. "Forever have the Mahars, who dwell beyond the Lidi Plains which lie at the farther rim of the Land of Awful Shadow, taken heavy toll of our people, whom they either force into life-long slavery or fatten for their feasts. We have heard that the great emperor makes successful war upon the Mahars, against whom we should be glad to fight.

"Recently has another reason come. Upon a great island which lies in the Sojar Az, but a short distance from our shores, a wicked man has collected a great band of outcast warriors of all tribes. Even are there many Sagoths among them, sent by the Mahars to aid the Wicked One.

"This band makes raids upon our villages, and it is constantly growing in size and strength, for the Mahars give liberty to any of their male prisoners who will promise to fight with this band against the enemies of the Mahars. It is the purpose of the Mahars thus to raise a force of our own kind to combat the growth and menace of the new empire of which I have come to seek information. All this we learned from one of our own warriors who had pretended to sympathize with this band and had then escaped at the first opportunity."

"Who could this man be," I asked Ghak, "who leads so vile a movement against his own kind?"

"His name is Hooja," spoke up Kolk, answering my question.

Ghak and I looked at each other. Relief was written upon his countenance and I know that it was beating strongly in my heart. At last we had discovered a tangible clue to the whereabouts of Hooja—and with the clue a guide!

But when I broached the subject to Kolk he demurred. He had

come a long way, he explained, to see his sister and to confer with Dacor. Moreover, he had instructions from his father which he could not ignore lightly. But even so he would return with me and show me the way to the island of the Thurian shore if by doing so we might accomplish anything.

"But we cannot," he urged. "Hooja is powerful. He has thousands of warriors. He has only to call upon his Mahar allies to receive a countless horde of Sagoths to do his bidding against his human enemies.

"Let us wait until you may gather an equal horde from the kingdoms of your empire. Then we may march against Hooja with some show of success.

"But first must you lure him to the mainland, for who among you knows how to construct the strange things that carry Hooja and his band back and forth across the water?

"We are not island people. We do not go upon the water. We know nothing of such things."

I couldn't persuade him to do more than direct me upon the way. I showed him my map, which now included a great area of country extending from Anoroc upon the east to Sari upon the west, and from the river south of the Mountains of the Clouds north to Amoz. As soon as I had explained it to him he drew a line with his finger, showing a sea-coast far to the west and south of Sari, and a great circle which he said marked the extent of the Land of Awful Shadow in which lay Thuria.

The shadow extended southeast of the coast out into the sea half-way to a large island, which he said was the seat of Hooja's traitorous government. The island itself lay in the light of the noonday sun. Northwest of the coast and embracing a part of Thuria lay the Lidi Plains, upon the northwestern verge of which was situated the Mahar city which took such heavy toll of the Thurians.

Thus were the unhappy people now between two fires, with Hooja upon one side and the Mahars upon the other. I did not wonder that they sent out an appeal for succor.

Though Ghak and Kolk both attempted to dissuade me, I was determined to set out at once, nor did I delay longer than to make a copy of my map to be given to Perry that he might add to his that which I had set down since we parted. I left a letter for him as well, in which among other things I advanced the theory that the Sojar Az, or Great Sea, which Kolk mentioned as stretching eastward from Thuria, might indeed be the same mighty ocean as that which, swinging around the southern end of a continent ran northward along the shore opposite Phutra, mingling its waters with the huge gulf upon which lay Sari, Amoz, and Greenwich.

Against this possibility I urged him to hasten the building of a fleet of small sailing-vessels, which we might utilize should I find it impossible to entice Hooja's horde to the mainland.

I told Ghak what I had written, and suggested that as soon as he could he should make new treaties with the various kingdoms of the empire, collect an army and march toward Thuria—this of course against the possibility of my detention through some cause or other.

Kolk gave me a sign to his father— a *lidi,* or beast of burden, crudely scratched upon a bit of bone, and beneath the lidi a man and a flower; all very rudely done perhaps, but none the less effective as I well knew from my long years among the primitive men of Pellucidar.

The lidi is the tribal beast of the Thurians; the man and the flower in the combination in which they appeared bore a double significance, as they constituted not only a message to the effect that the bearer came in peace, but were also Kolk's signature.

And so, armed with my credentials and my small arsenal, I set out alone upon my quest for the dearest girl in this world or yours.

Kolk gave me explicit directions, though with my map I do not believe that I could have gone wrong. As a matter of fact I did not need the map at all, since the principal landmark of the first half of my journey, a gigantic mountain-peak, was plainly visible from Sari, though a good hundred miles away.

At the southern base of this mountain a river rose and ran in a westerly direction, finally turning south and emptying into the Sojar Az some forty miles northeast of Thuria. All that I had to do was follow this river to the sea and then follow the coast to Thuria.

Two hundred and forty miles of wild mountain and primeval jungle, of untracked plain, of nameless rivers, of deadly swamps and savage forests lay ahead of me, yet never had I been more eager for an adventure than now, for never had more depended upon haste and success.

I do not know how long a time that journey required, and only half did I appreciate the varied wonders that each new march unfolded before me, for my mind and heart were filled with but a single image—that of a perfect girl whose great, dark eyes looked bravely forth from a frame of raven hair.

It was not until I had passed the high peak and found the river that my eyes first discovered the pendent world, the tiny satellite which hangs low over the surface of Pellucidar casting its perpetual shadow always upon the same spot—the area that is known here as the Land of Awful Shadow, in which dwells the tribe of Thuria.

From the distance and the elevation of the highlands where I stood the Pellucidarian noonday moon showed half in sunshine and half in shadow, while directly beneath it was plainly visible the round dark spot upon the surface of Pellucidar where the sun has never shone. From where I stood the moon appeared to hang so low above the ground as almost to touch it; but later I was to learn that it floats a mile above the surface—which seems indeed quite close for a moon.

Following the river downward I soon lost sight of the tiny planet as I entered the mazes of a lofty forest. Nor did I catch another glimpse of it for some time—several marches at least. However, when the river led me to the sea, or rather just before it reached the sea, of a sudden the sky became overcast and the size and luxuriance of the vegetation diminished as by magic—as if an omnipotent hand had drawn a line upon the earth, and said:

"Upon this side shall the trees and the shrubs, the grasses and the flowers, riot in profusion of rich colors, gigantic size and bewildering abundance; and upon that side shall they be dwarfed and pale and scant."

Instantly I looked above, for clouds are so uncommon in the skies of Pellucidar—they are practically unknown except above the mightiest mountain ranges—that it had given me something of a start to discover the sun obliterated. But I was not long in coming to a realization of the cause of the shadow.

Above me hung another world. I could see its mountains and valleys, oceans, lakes, and rivers, its broad, grassy plains and dense forests. But too great was the distance and too deep the shadow of its under side for me to distinguish any movement as of animal life.

Instantly a great curiosity was awakened within me. The questions which the sight of this planet, so tantalizingly close, raised in my mind were numerous and unanswerable.

Was it inhabited?

If so, by what manner and form of creature?

Were its people as relatively diminutive as their little world, or were they as disproportionately huge as the lesser attraction of gravity upon the surface of their globe would permit of their being?

As I watched it, I saw that it was revolving upon an axis that lay parallel to the surface of Pellucidar, so that during each revolution its entire surface was once exposed to the world below and once bathed in the heat of the great sun above. The little world had that which Pellucidar could not have—a day and night, and—greatest of boons to one outer-earthly born—time.

Here I saw a chance to give time to Pellucidar, using this mighty clock, revolving perpetually in the heavens, to record the passage of the hours for the earth below. Here should be located an observatory, from which might be flashed by wireless to every corner of the empire the correct time once each day. That this time would be easily measured I had no doubt, since so plain were the landmarks upon the under surface of the satellite that it would be but necessary to erect a simple instrument and mark the instant of passage of a given landmark across the instrument.

But then was not the time for dreaming; I must devote my time to the purpose of my journey. So I hastened onward beneath the great shadow. As I advanced I could not but note the changing nature of the vegetation and the paling of its hues.

The river led me a short distance within the shadow before it emptied into the Sojar Az. Then I continued in a southerly direction along the coast toward the village of Thuria, where I hoped to find Goork and deliver to him my credentials.

I had progressed no great distance from the mouth of the river when I discerned, lying some distance at sea, a great island. This I assumed to be the stronghold of Hooja, nor did I doubt that upon it even now was Dian.

The way was most difficult, since shortly after leaving the river I encountered lofty cliffs split by numerous long, narrow fiords, each of which necessitated a considerable detour. As the crow flies it is about twenty miles from the mouth of the river to Thuria, but before I had covered half of it I was fagged. There was no familiar fruit or vegetable growing upon the rocky soil of the cliff-tops, and I would have fared ill for food had not a hare broken cover almost beneath my nose.

I carried bow and arrows to conserve my ammunition-supply, but so quick was the little animal that I had no time to draw and fit a shaft. In fact my dinner was a hundred yards away and going like the proverbial bat when I dropped my six-shooter on it. It was a pretty shot and when coupled with a good dinner made me quite contented with myself.

After eating I lay down and slept. When I awoke I was scarcely so self-satisfied, for I had not more than opened my eyes before I became aware of the presence, barely a hundred yards from me, of a pack of some twenty huge wolf-dogs—the things which Perry

insisted upon calling hyaenodons—and almost simultaneously I
discovered that while I slept my revolvers, rifle, bow, arrows, and
knife had been stolen from me.

And the wolf-dog pack was preparing to rush me.

CHAPTER VII

FROM PLIGHT TO PLIGHT

I HAVE never been much of a runner; I hate running. But if ever
a sprinter broke into smithereens all world's records it was I that
day when I fled before those hideous beasts along the narrow spit
of rocky cliff between two narrow fiords toward the Sojar Az. Just
as I reached the verge of the cliff the foremost of the brutes was
upon me. He leaped and closed his massive jaws upon my shoulder.

The momentum of his flying body, added to that of my own,
carried the two of us over the cliff. It was a hideous fall. The cliff
was almost perpendicular. At its foot broke the sea against a solid
wall of rock.

We struck the cliff-face once in our descent and then plunged
into the salt sea. With the impact with the water the hyaenodon
released his hold upon my shoulder.

As I came sputtering to the surface I looked about for some tiny
foot- or hand-hold where I might cling for a moment of rest and
recuperation. The cliff itself offered me nothing, so I swam toward
the mouth of the fiord.

At the far end I could see that erosion from above had washed
down sufficient rubble to form a narrow ribbon of beach. Toward
this I swam with all my strength. Not once did I look behind me,
since every unnecessary movement in swimming detracts so much
from one's endurance and speed. Not until I had drawn myself
safely out upon the beach did I turn my eyes back toward the sea
for the hyaenodon. He was swimming slowly and apparently pain-
fully toward the beach upon which I stood.

I watched him for a long time, wondering why it was that such
a doglike animal was not a better swimmer. As he neared me I
realized that he was weakening rapidly. I had gathered a handful
of stones to be ready for his assault when he landed, but in a
moment I let them fall from my hands. It was evident that the

brute either was no swimmer or else was severely injured, for by now he was making practically no headway. Indeed, it was with quite apparent difficulty that he kept his nose above the surface of the sea.

He was not more than fifty yards from shore when he went under. I watched the spot where he had disappeared, and in a moment I saw his head reappear. The look of dumb misery in his eyes struck a chord in my breast, for I love dogs. I forgot that he was a vicious, primordial wolf-thing—a man-eater, a scourge, and a terror. I saw only the sad eyes that looked like the eyes of Raja, my dead collie of the outer world.

I did not stop to weigh and consider. In other words, I did not stop to think, which I believe must be the way of men who do things—in contradistinction to those who think much and do nothing. Instead, I leaped back into the water and swam out toward the drowning beast. At first he showed his teeth at my approach, but just before I reached him he went under for the second time, so that I had to dive to get him.

I grabbed him by the scruff of the neck, and though he weighed as much as a Shetland pony, I managed to drag him to shore and well up upon the beach. Here I found that one of his forelegs was broken—the crash against the cliff-face must have done it.

By this time all the fight was out of him, so that when I had gathered a few tiny branches from some of the stunted trees that grew in the crevices of the cliff, and returned to him he permitted me to set his broken leg and bind it in splints. I had to tear part of my shirt into bits to obtain a bandage, but at last the job was done. Then I sat stroking the savage head and talking to the beast in the man-dog talk with which you are familiar, if you ever owned and loved a dog.

When he is well, I thought, he probably will turn upon me and attempt to devour me, and against that eventuality I gathered together a pile of rocks and set to work to fashion a stone-knife. We were bottled up at the head of that fiord as completely as if we had been behind prison bars. Before us spread the Sojar Az, and elsewhere about us rose unscalable cliffs.

Fortunately a little rivulet trickled down the side of the rocky wall, giving us ample supply of fresh water—some of which I kept constantly beside the hyaenodon in a huge, bowl-shaped shell, of which there were countless numbers among the rubble of the beach.

For food we subsisted upon shell-fish and an occasional bird that I succeeded in knocking over with a rock, for long practice as a pitcher on prep-school and varsity nines had made me an excellent shot with a hand-thrown missile.

It was not long before the hyaenodon's leg was sufficiently mended to permit him to rise and hobble about on three legs. I shall never forget with what intent interest I watched his first attempt. Close at my hand lay my pile of rocks. Slowly the beast came to his three good feet. He stretched himself, lowered his head, and lapped water from the drinking-shell at his side, turned and looked at me, and then hobbled off toward the cliffs.

Thrice he traversed the entire extent of our prison, seeking, I imagine, a loop-hole for escape, but finding none he returned in my direction. Slowly he came quite close to me, sniffed at my shoes, my puttees, my hands, and then limped off a few feet and lay down again.

Now that he was able to get around, I was a little uncertain as to the wisdom of my impulsive mercy.

How could I sleep with that ferocious thing prowling about the narrow confines of our prison?

Should I close my eyes it might be to open them again to the feel of those mighty jaws at my throat. To say the least, I was uncomfortable.

I have had too much experience with dumb animals to bank very strongly on any sense of gratitude which may be attributed to them by inexperienced sentimentalists. I believe that some animals love their masters, but I doubt very much if their affection is the outcome of gratitude—a characteristic that is so rare as to be only occasionally traceable in the seemingly unselfish acts of man himself.

But finally I was forced to sleep. Tired nature would be put off no longer. I simply fell asleep, willy nilly, as I sat looking out to sea. I had been very uncomfortable since my ducking in the ocean, for though I could see the sunlight on the water half-way out toward the island and upon the island itself, no ray of it fell upon us. We were well within the Land of Awful Shadow. A perpetual half-warmth pervaded the atmosphere, but clothing was slow in drying, and so from loss of sleep and great physical discomfort, I at last gave way to nature's demands and sank into profound slumber.

When I awoke it was with a start, for a heavy body was upon me. My first thought was that the hyaenodon had at last attacked me, but as my eyes opened and I struggled to rise, I saw that a man was astride me and three others bending close above him.

I am no weakling—and never have been. My experience in the

hard life of the inner world has turned my thews to steel. Even such giants as Ghak the Hairy One have praised my strength; but to it is added another quality which they lack—science.

The man upon me held me down awkwardly, leaving me many openings—one of which I was not slow in taking advantage of, so that almost before the fellow knew that I was awake I was upon my feet with my arms over his shoulders and about his waist and had hurled him heavily over my head to the hard rubble of the beach, where he lay quite still.

In the instant that I arose I had seen the hyaenodon lying asleep beside a boulder a few yards away. So nearly was he the color of the rock that he was scarcely discernible. Evidently the newcomers had not seen him.

I had not more than freed myself from one of my antagonists before the other three were upon me. They did not work silently now, but charged me with savage cries—a mistake upon their part. The fact that they did not draw their weapons against me convinced me that they desired to take me alive; but I fought as desperately as if death loomed immediate and sure.

The battle was short, for scarce had their first wild whoop reverberated through the rocky fiord, and they had closed upon me, than a hairy mass of demoniacal rage hurtled among us.

It was the hyaenodon!

In an instant he had pulled down one of the men, and with a single shake, terrier-like, had broken his neck. Then he was upon another. In their efforts to vanquish the wolf-dog the savages forgot all about me, thus giving me an instant in which to snatch a knife from the loin-string of him who had first fallen and account for another of them. Almost simultaneously the hyaenodon pulled down the remaining enemy, crushing his skull with a single bite of those fearsome jaws.

The battle was over—unless the beast considered me fair prey, too. I waited, ready for him with knife and bludgeon—also filched from a dead foeman; but he paid no attention to me, falling to work instead to devour one of the corpses.

The beast had been handicapped but little by his splinted leg; but having eaten he lay down and commenced to gnaw at the bandage. I was sitting some little distance away devouring shellfish, of which, by the way, I was becoming exceedingly tired.

Presently the hyaenodon arose and came toward me. I did not move. He stopped in front of me and deliberately raised his bandaged leg and pawed my knee. His act was as intelligible as words —he wished the bandage removed.

I took the great paw in one hand and with the other untied and unwound the bandage, removed the splints and felt of the injured member. As far as I could judge the bone was completely knit. The joint was stiff; when I bent it a little the brute winced—but he neither growled nor tried to pull away. Very slowly and gently I rubbed the joint and applied pressure to it for a few moments.

Then I set it down upon the ground. The hyaenodon walked around me a few times, and then lay down at my side, his body touching mine. I laid my hand upon his head. He did not move. Slowly I scratched about his ears and neck and down beneath the fierce jaws. The only sign he gave was to raise his chin a trifle that I might better caress him.

That was enough! From that moment I have never again felt suspicion of Raja, as I immediately named him. Somehow all sense of loneliness vanished, too—I had a dog! I had never guessed precisely what it was that was lacking to life in Pellucidar, but now I knew that it was the total absence of domestic animals.

Men here had not yet reached the point where he might take the time from slaughter and escaping slaughter to make friends with any of the brute creation. I must qualify this statement a trifle and say that this was true of those tribes with which I was most familiar. The Thurians do domesticate the colossal lidi, traversing the great Lidi Plains upon the backs of these grotesque and stupendous monsters, and possibly there may also be other, far-distant peoples within this great world, who have tamed others of the wild things of jungle, plain or mountain.

The Thurians practice agriculture in a crude sort of way. It is my opinion that this is one of the earliest steps from savagery to civilization. The taming of wild beasts and their domestication follows.

Perry argues that wild dogs were first domesticated for hunting purposes; but I do not agree with him. I believe that if their domestication were not purely the result of an accident, as, for example, my taming of the hyaenodon, it came about through the desire of tribes who had previously domesticated flocks and herds to have some strong, ferocious beast to guard their roaming property. However, I lean rather more strongly to the theory of accident.

As I sat there upon the beach of the little fiord eating my unpalatable shellfish, I commenced to wonder how it had been that the four savages had been able to reach me, though I had been unable to escape from my natural prison. I glanced about in all directions, searching for an explanation. At last my eyes fell upon the bow of a small dugout protruding scarce a foot from behind a large boulder lying half in the water at the edge of the beach.

At my discovery I leaped to my feet so suddenly that it brought Raja, growling and bristling, upon all fours in an instant. For the moment I had forgotten him. But his savage rumbling did not cause me any uneasiness. He glanced quickly about in all directions as if searching for the cause of my excitement. Then, as I walked rapidly down toward the dugout, he slunk silently after me.

The dugout was similar in many respects to those which I had seen in use by the Mezops. In it were four paddles. I was much delighted, as it promptly offered me the escape I had been craving.

I pushed it out into water that would float it, stepped in and called to Raja to enter. At first he did not seem to understand what I wished of him, but after I had paddled out a few yards he plunged through the surf and swam after me. When he had come alongside I grasped the scruff of his neck, and after a considerable struggle, in which I several times came near to overturning the canoe, I managed to drag him aboard, where he shook himself vigorously and squatted down before me.

After emerging from the fiord, I paddled southward along the coast, where presently the lofty cliffs gave way to lower and more level country. It was here somewhere that I should come upon the principal village of the Thurians. When, after a time, I saw in the distance what I took to be huts in a clearing near the shore, I drew quickly into land, for though I had been furnished with credentials by Kolk, I was not sufficiently familiar with the tribal characteristics of these people to know whether I should receive a friendly welcome or not; and in case I should not, I wanted to be sure of having a canoe hidden safely away so that I might undertake the trip to the island, in any event—provided, of course, that I escaped the Thurians should they prove belligerent.

At the point where I landed the shore was quite low. A forest of pale, scrubby ferns ran down almost to the beach. Here I dragged up the dugout, hiding it well within the vegetation, and with some loose rocks built a cairn upon the beach to mark my cache. Then I turned my steps toward the Thurian village.

As I proceeded I began to speculate upon the possible actions of Raja when we should enter the presence of other men than myself. The brute was padding softly at my side, his sensitive nose constantly atwitch and his fierce eyes moving restlessly from side to side—nothing would ever take Raja unawares!

The more I thought upon the matter the greater became my

perturbation. I did not want Raja to attack any of the people upon whose friendship I so greatly depended, nor did I want him injured or slain by them.

I wondered if Raja would stand for a leash. His head as he paced beside me was level with my hip. I laid my hand upon it, caressingly. As I did so he turned and looked up into my face, his jaws parting and his red tongue lolling as you have seen your own dog's beneath a love pat.

"Just been waiting all your life to be tamed and loved, haven't you, old man?" I asked. "You're nothing but a good old pup, and the man who put the hyaeno in your name ought to be sued for libel."

Raja bared his mighty fangs with upcurled, snarling lips and licked my hand.

"You're grinning, you old fraud, you!" I cried. "If you're not, I'll eat you. I'll bet a doughnut you're nothing but some kid's poor old Fido, masquerading around as a real, live man-eater."

Raja whined. And so we walked on together toward Thuria—I talking to the beast at my side, and he seeming to enjoy my company no less than I enjoyed his. If you don't think it's lonesome wandering all by yourself through savage, unknown Pellucidar, why, just try it, and you will not wonder that I was glad of the company of this first dog—this living replica of the fierce and now extinct hyaenodon of the outer crust that hunted in savage packs the great elk across the snows of southern France, in the days when the mastodon roamed at will over the broad continent of which the British Isles were then a part, and perchance left his footprints and his bones in the sands of Atlantis as well.

Thus I dreamed as we moved on toward Thuria. My dreaming was rudely shattered by a savage growl from Raja. I looked down at him. He had stopped in his tracks as one turned to stone. A thin ridge of stiff hair bristled along the entire length of his spine. His yellow-green eyes were fastened upon the scrubby jungle at our right.

I fastened my fingers in the bristles at his neck and turned my eyes in the direction that his pointed. At first I saw nothing. Then a slight movement of the bushes riveted my attention. I thought it must be some wild beast, and was glad of the primitive weapons I had taken from the bodies of the warriors who had attacked me.

Presently I distinguished two eyes peering at us from the vegetation. I took a step in their direction, and as I did so a youth arose and fled precipitately in the direction we had been going. Raja struggled to be after him, but I held tightly to his neck, an act which he did not seem to relish, for he turned on me with bared fangs.

I determined that now was as good a time as any to discover just how deep was Raja's affection for me. One of us must be master, and logically I was the one. He growled at me. I cuffed him sharply across the nose. He looked at me for a moment in surprised bewilderment, and then he growled again. I made another feint at him, expecting that it would bring him at my throat; but instead he winced and crouched down.

Raja was subdued!

I stooped and patted him. Then I took a piece of the rope that constituted a part of my equipment and made a leash for him.

Thus we resumed our journey toward Thuria. The youth who had seen us was evidently of the Thurians. That he had lost no time in racing homeward and spreading the word of my coming was evidenced when we had come within sight of the clearing, and the village—the first real village, by the way, that I had ever seen constructed by human Pellucidarians. There was a rude rectangle walled with logs and boulders, in which were a hundred or more thatched huts of similar construction. There was no gate. Ladders that could be removed by night led over the palisade.

Before the village were assembled a great concourse of warriors. Inside I could see the heads of women and children peering over the top of the wall; and also, farther back, the long necks of lidi, topped by their tiny heads. Lidi, by the way, is both the singular and plural form of the noun that describes the huge beasts of burden of the Thurians. They are enormous quadrupeds, eighty or a hundred feet long, with very small heads perched at the top of very long, slender necks. Their heads are quite forty feet from the ground. Their gait is slow and deliberate, but so enormous are their strides that, as a matter of fact, they cover the ground quite rapidly.

Perry has told me that they are almost identical with the fossilized remains of the diplodocus of the outer crust's Jurassic age. I have to take his word for it—and I guess you will, unless you know more of such matters than I.

As we came in sight of the warriors the men set up a great jabbering. Their eyes were wide in astonishment—not only, I presume, because of my strange garmenture, but as well from the fact that I came in company with a jalok, which is the Pellucidarian name of the hyaenodon.

Raja tugged at his leash, growling and showing his long white fangs. He would have liked nothing better than to be at the throats of the whole aggregation; but I held him in with the leash, though it took all my strength to do it. My free hand I held above my head, palm out, in token of the peacefulness of my mission.

In the foreground I saw the youth who had discovered us, and I could tell from the way he carried himself that he was quite overcome by his own importance. The warriors about him were all fine looking fellows, though shorter and squatter than the Sarians or the Amozites. Their color, too, was a bit lighter, owing, no doubt, to the fact that much of their lives is spent within the shadow of the world that hangs forever above their country.

A little in advance of the others was a bearded fellow tricked out in many ornaments. I didn't need to ask to know that he was the chieftain—doubtless Goork, father of Kolk. Now to him I addressed myself.

"I am David," I said, "Emperor of the Federated Kingdoms of Pellucidar. Doubtless you have heard of me?"

He nodded his head affirmatively.

"I come from Sari," I continued, "where I just met Kolk, the son of Goork. I bear a token from Kolk to his father, which will prove that I am a friend."

Again the warrior nodded. "I am Goork," he said. "Where is the token?"

"Here," I replied, and fished into the game-bag where I had placed it.

Goork and his people waited in silence. My hand searched the inside of the bag.

It was empty!

The token had been stolen with my arms!

CHAPTER VIII

CAPTIVE

WHEN Goork and his people saw that I had no token they commenced to taunt me.

"You do not come from Kolk, but from the Sly One!" they cried. "He has sent you from the island to spy upon us. Go away, or we will set upon you and kill you."

I explained that all my belongings had been stolen from me,

and that the robber must have taken the token, too; but they didn't believe me. As proof that I was one of Hooja's people, they pointed to my weapons, which they said were ornamented like those of the island clan. Further, they said that no good man went in company with a jalok—and that by this line of reasoning I certainly was a bad man.

I saw that they were not naturally a warlike tribe, for they preferred that I leave in peace rather than force them to attack me, whereas the Sarians would have killed a suspicious stranger first and inquired into his purposes later.

I think Raja sensed their antagonism, for he kept tugging at his leash and growling ominously. They were a bit in awe of him, and kept at a safe distance. It was evident that they could not comprehend why it was that this savage brute did not turn upon me and rend me.

I wasted a long time there trying to persuade Goork to accept me at my own valuation, but he was too canny. The best he would do was to give us food, which he did, and direct me as to the safest portion of the island upon which to attempt a landing, though even as he told me I am sure that he thought my request for information but a blind to deceive him as to my true knowledge of the insular stronghold.

At last I turned away from them—rather disheartened, for I had hoped to be able to enlist a considerable force of them in an attempt to rush Hooja's horde and rescue Dian. Back along the beach toward the hidden canoe we made our way.

By the time we came to the cairn I was dog-tired. Throwing myself upon the sand I soon slept, and with Raja stretched out beside me I felt a far greater security than I had enjoyed for a long time.

I awoke much refreshed to find Raja's eyes glued upon me. The moment I opened mine he rose, stretched himself, and without a backward glance plunged into the jungle. For several minutes I could hear him crashing through the brush. Then all was silent.

I wondered if he had left me to return to his fierce pack. A feeling of loneliness overwhelmed me. With a sigh I turned to the work of dragging the canoe down to the sea. As I entered the jungle where the dugout lay a hare darted from beneath the boat's side, and a well-aimed cast of my javelin brought it down. I was hungry— I had not realized it before—so I sat upon the edge of the canoe and devoured my repast. The last remnants gone, I again busied myself with preparations for my expedition to the island.

I did not know for certain that Dian was there; but I surmised

as much. Nor could I guess what obstacles might confront me in
an effort to rescue her. For a time I loitered about after I had the
canoe at the water's edge, hoping against hope that Raja would
return; but he did not, so I shoved the awkward craft through the
surf and leaped into it.

I was still a little downcast by the desertion of my new-found
friend, though I tried to assure myself that it was nothing but
what I might have expected.

The savage brute had served me well in the short time that we
had been together, and had repaid his debt of gratitude to me,
since he had saved my life, or at least my liberty, no less certainly
than I had saved his life when he was injured and drowning.

The trip across the water to the island was uneventful. I was
mighty glad to be in the sunshine again when I passed out of the
shadow of the dead world about half-way between the mainland
and the island. The hot rays of the noonday sun did a great deal
toward raising my spirits, and dispelling the mental gloom in
which I had been shrouded almost continually since entering the
Land of Awful Shadow. There is nothing more dispiriting to me
than absence of sunshine.

I had paddled to the southwestern point, which Goork said he
believed to be the least frequented portion of the island, as he had
never seen boats put off from there. I found a shallow reef running far out into the sea and rather precipitous cliffs running
almost to the surf. It was a nasty place to land, and I realized now
why it was not used by the natives; but at last I managed, after a
good wetting, to beach my canoe and scale the cliffs.

The country beyond them appeared more open and parklike
than I had anticipated, since from the mainland the entire coast
that is visible seems densely clothed with tropical jungle. This
jungle, as I could see from the vantage-point of the cliff-top, formed
but a relatively narrow strip between the sea and the more open
forest and meadow of the interior. Farther back there was a range
of low but apparently very rocky hills, and here and there all about
were visible flat-topped masses of rock—small mountains, in fact—
which reminded me of pictures I had seen of landscapes in New
Mexico. Altogether, the country was very much broken and very
beautiful. From where I stood I counted no less than a dozen
streams winding down from among the table-buttes and emptying into a pretty river which flowed away in a northeasterly direction toward the opposite end of the island.

As I let my eyes roam over the scene I suddenly became aware
of figures moving upon the flat top of a far-distant butte. Whether

they were beast or human, though, I could not make out; but at least they were alive, so I determined to prosecute my search for Hooja's stronghold in the general direction of this butte.

To descend to the valley required no great effort. As I swung along through the lush grass and the fragrant flowers, my cudgel swinging in my hand and my javelin looped across my shoulders with its aurochs-hide strap, I felt equal to any emergency, ready for any danger.

I had covered quite a little distance, and I was passing through a strip of wood which lay at the foot of one of the flat-topped hills, when I became conscious of the sensation of being watched. My life within Pellucidar has rather quickened my senses of sight, hearing, and smell, and, too, certain primitive intuitive or instinctive qualities that seem blunted in civilized man. But, though I was positive that eyes were upon me, I could see no sign of any living thing within the wood other than the many, gay-plumaged birds and little monkeys which filled the trees with life, color, and action.

To you it may seem that my conviction was the result of an over-wrought imagination, or to the actual reality of the prying eyes of the little monkeys or the curious ones of the birds; but there is a difference which I cannot explain between the sensation of casual observation and studied espionage. A sheep might gaze at you without transmitting a warning through your subjective mind, because you are in no danger from a sheep. But let a tiger gaze fixedly at you from ambush, and unless your primitive instincts are completely calloused you will presently commence to glance furtively about and be filled with vague, unreasoning terror.

Thus was it with me then. I grasped my cudgel more firmly and unslung my javelin, carrying it in my left hand. I peered to left and right, but I saw nothing. Then, all quite suddenly, there fell about my neck and shoulders, around my arms and body, a number of pliant fiber ropes.

In a jiffy I was trussed up as neatly as you might wish. One of the nooses dropped to my ankles and was jerked up with a sudden-ness that brought me to my face upon the ground. Then something heavy and hairy sprang upon my back. I fought to draw my knife, but hairy hands grasped my wrists and, dragging them behind my back, bound them securely.

Next my feet were bound. Then I was turned over upon my back to look up into the faces of my captors.

And what faces! Imagine if you can a cross between a sheep and a gorilla, and you will have some conception of the physiognomy of the creature that bent close above me, and of those of the half-dozen others that clustered about. There was the facial length and great eyes of the sheep, and the bull-neck and hideous fangs of the gorilla. The bodies and limbs were both man- and gorilla-like.

As they bent over me they conversed in a monosyllabic tongue that was perfectly intelligible to me. It was something of a simplified language that had no need for aught but nouns and verbs, but such words as it included were the same as those of the human beings of Pellucidar. It was amplified by many gestures which filled in the speech-gaps.

I asked them what they intended doing with me; but, like our own North American Indians when questioned by a white man, they pretended not to understand me. One of them swung me to his shoulder as lightly as if I had been a shoat. He was a huge creature, as were his fellows, standing fully seven feet upon his short legs and weighing considerably more than a quarter of a ton.

Two went ahead of my bearer and three behind. In this order we cut to the right through the forest to the foot of the hill where precipitous cliffs appeared to bar our farther progress in this direction. But my escort never paused. Like ants upon a wall, they scaled that seemingly unscalable barrier, clinging, Heaven knows how, to its ragged, perpendicular face. During most of the short journey to the summit I must admit that my hair stood on end. Presently, however, we topped the thing and stood upon the level mesa which crowned it.

Immediately from all about, out of burrows and rough, rocky lairs, poured a perfect torrent of beasts similar to my captors. They clustered about, jabbering at my guards and attempting to get their hands upon me, whether from curosity or a desire to do me bodily harm I did not know, since my escort with bared fangs and heavy blows kept them off.

Across the mesa we went, to stop at last before a large pile of rocks in which an opening appeared. Here my guards set me upon my feet and called out a word which sounded like "Gr-gr-gr!" and which I later learned was the name of their king.

Presently there emerged from the cavernous depth of the lair a monstrous creature, scarred from a hundred battles, almost hairless and with an empty socket where one eye had been. The other eye, sheeplike in its mildness, gave the most startling appearance to the beast, which but for that single timid orb was the most fearsome thing that one could imagine.

I had encountered the black, hairless, long-tailed ape-things of the mainland—the creatures which Perry thought might constitute the link between the higher orders of apes and man—but these brute-men of Gr-gr-gr seemed to set that theory back to zero, for there was less similarity between the black ape-men and these creatures than there was between the latter and man, while both had many human attributes, some of which were better developed in one species and some in the other.

The black apes were hairless and built thatched huts in their arboreal retreats; they kept domesticated dogs and ruminants, in which respect they were farther advanced than the human beings of Pellucidar; but they appeared to have only a meager language, and sported long, apelike tails.

On the other hand, Gr-gr-gr's people were, for the most part, quite hairy, but they were tailless and had a language similar to that of the human race of Pellucidar; nor were they aboreal. Their skins, where skin showed, were white.

From the foregoing facts and others that I have noted during my long life within Pellucidar, which is now passing through an age analogous to some preglacial age of the outer crust, I am constrained to the belief that evolution is not so much a gradual transition from one form to another as it is an accident of breeding, either by crossing or the hazards of birth. In other words, it is my belief that the first man was a freak of nature—nor would one have to draw over-strongly upon his credulity to be convinced that Gr-gr-gr and his tribe were also freaks.

The great man-brute seated himself upon a flat rock—his throne, I imagine—just before the entrance to his lair. With elbows on knees and chin in palms he regarded me intently through his lone sheep-eye while one of my captors told of my taking.

When all had been related Gr-gr-gr questioned me. I shall not attempt to quote these people in their own abbreviated tongue— you would have even greater difficulty in interpreting them than did I. Instead, I shall put the words into their mouths which will carry to you the ideas which they intended to convey.

"You are an enemy," was Gr-gr-gr's initial declaration. "You belong to the tribe of Hooja."

Ah! So they knew Hooja and he was their enemy! Good!

"I am an enemy of Hooja," I replied. "He has stolen my mate and I have come here to take her away from him and punish Hooja."

"How could you do that alone?"

"I do not know," I answered, "but I should have tried had you not captured me. What do you intend to do with me?"

"You shall work for us."

"You will not kill me?" I asked.

"We do not kill except in self-defense," he replied; "self-defense and punishment. Those who would kill us and those who do wrong we kill. If we knew that you were one of Hooja's people we might kill you, for all Hooja's people are bad people; but you say you are an enemy of Hooja. You may not speak the truth, but until we learn that you have lied we shall not kill you. You shall work."

"If you hate Hooja," I suggested, "why not let me, who hate him, too, go and punish him?"

For some time Gr-gr-gr sat in thought. Then he raised his head and addressed my guard.

"Take him to his work," he ordered.

His tone was final. As if to emphasize it he turned and entered his burrow. My guard conducted me farther into the mesa, where we came presently to a tiny depression or valley, at one end of which gushed a warm spring.

The view that opened before me was the most surprising that I have ever seen. In the hollow, which must have covered several hundred acres, were numerous fields of growing things, and working all about with crude implements or with no implements at all other than their bare hands were many of the brute-men engaged in the first agriculture that I had seen within Pellucidar.

They put me to work cultivating in a patch of melons. I never was a farmer nor particularly keen for this sort of work, and I am free to confess that time never had dragged so heavily as it did during the hour or the year I spent there at that work. How long it really was I do not know, of course; but it was all too long.

The creatures that worked about me were quite simple and friendly. One of them proved to be a son of Gr-gr-gr. He had broken some minor tribal law, and was working out his sentence in the fields. He told me that his tribe had lived upon this hilltop always, and that there were other tribes like them dwelling upon other hilltops. They had no wars and had always lived in peace and harmony, menaced only by the larger carnivora of the island, until my kind had come under a creature called Hooja, and attacked and killed them when they chanced to descend from their natural fortresses to visit their fellows upon other lofty mesas.

Now they were afraid; but some day they would go in a body and fall upon Hooja and his people and slay them all. I explained to him that I was Hooja's enemy, and asked, when they were ready to go, that I be allowed to go with them, or, better still, that they let me go ahead and learn all that I could about the village where

Hooja dwelt so that they might attack it with the best chance of success.

Gr-gr-gr's son seemed much impressed by my suggestion. He said that when he was through in the fields he would speak to his father about the matter.

Some time after this Gr-gr-gr came through the fields where we were, and his son spoke to him upon the subject, but the old gentleman was evidently in anything but a good humor, for he cuffed the youngster and, turning upon me, informed me that he was convinced that I had lied to him, and that I was one of Hooja's people.

"Wherefore," he concluded, "we shall slay you as soon as the melons are cultivated. Hasten, therefore."

And hasten I did. I hastened to cultivate the weeds which grew among the melon-vines. Where there had been one sickly weed before, I nourished two healthy ones. When I found a particularly promising variety of weed growing elsewhere than among my melons, I forthwith dug it up and transplanted. it among my charges.

My masters did not seem to realize my perfidy. They saw me always laboring diligently in the melon-patch, and as time enters not into the reckoning of Pellucidarians—even of human beings and much less of brutes and half-brutes—I might have lived on indefinitely through this subterfuge had not that occurred which took me out of the melon-patch for good and all.

CHAPTER IX

HOOJA'S CUTTHROATS APPEAR

I HAD built a little shelter of rocks and brush where I might crawl in and sleep out of the perpetual light and heat of the noonday sun. When I was tired or hungry I retired to my humble cot.

My masters never interposed the slightest objection. As a matter of fact, they were very good to me, nor did I see aught while I was among them to indicate that they are ever else than a simple, kindly folk when left to themselves. Their awe-inspiring size, terrific strength, mighty fighting-fangs, and hideous appearance are but the attributes necessary to the successful waging of their con-

stant battle for survival, and well do they employ them when the
need arises. The only flesh they eat is that of herbivorous animals
and birds. When they hunt the mighty thag, the prehistoric bos
of the outer crust, a single male, with his fiber rope, will catch and
kill the greatest of the bulls.

Well, as I was about to say, I had this little shelter at the edge
of my melon-patch. Here I was resting from my labors on a certain
occasion when I heard a great hubbub in the village, which lay
about a quarter of a mile away.

Presently a male came racing toward the field, shouting excitedly.
As he approached I came from my shelter to learn what all the
commotion might be about, for the monotony of my existence in
the melon-patch must have fostered that trait of curiosity from
which it had always been my secret boast that I am peculiarly free.

The other workers also ran forward to meet the messenger, who
quickly unburdened himself of his information, and as quickly
turned and scampered back toward the village. When running
these beast-men often go upon all fours. Thus they leap over obstacles that would slow up a human being, and upon the level
attain a speed that would make a thoroughbred look to his laurels.
The result in this instance was that before I had more than assimi-
lated the gist of the word which had been brought to the fields,
I was alone, watching my erstwhile co-workers speeding village-
ward.

I was alone! It was the first time since my capture that no beast-
man had been within sight of me. I was alone! And all my captors
were in the village at the opposite edge of the mesa repelling an
attack of Hooja's horde!

It seemed from the messenger's tale that two of Gr-gr-gr's great
males had been set upon by a half-dozen of Hooja's cutthroats
while the former were peaceably returning from the thag hunt. The
two had returned to the village unscratched, while but a single
one of Hooja's half-dozen had escaped to report the outcome of
the battle to their leader. Now Hooja was coming to punish
Gr-gr-gr's people. With his large force, armed with the bows and
arrows that Hooja had learned from me to make, with long lances
and sharp knives, I feared that even the mighty strength of the
beast-men could avail them but little.

At last had come the opportunity for which I waited! I was free
to make for the far end of the mesa, find my way to the valley
below, and while the two forces were engaged in their struggle,
continue my search for Hooja's village, which I had learned from

the beast-men lay further on down the river that I had been following when taken prisoner.

As I turned to make for the mesa's rim the sounds of battle came plainly to my ears—the hoarse shouts of men mingled with the half-beastly roars and growls of the brute-folk.

Did I take advantage of my opportunity?

I did not. Instead, lured by the din of strife and by the desire to deliver a stroke, however feeble, against hated Hooja, I wheeled and ran directly toward the village.

When I reached the edge of the plateau such a scene met my astonished gaze as never before had startled it, for the unique battle-methods of the half-brutes were rather the most remarkable I had ever witnessed. Along the very edge of the cliff-top stood a thin line of mighty males—the best rope-throwers of the tribe. A few feet behind these the rest of the males, with the exception of about twenty, formed a second line. Still farther in the rear all the women and young children were clustered into a single group under the protection of the remaining twenty fighting males and all the old males.

But it was the work of the first two lines that interested me. The forces of Hooja—a great horde of savage Sagoths and primeval cave men—were working their way up the steep cliff-face, their agility but slightly less than that of my captors who had clambered so nimbly aloft—even he who was burdened by my weight.

As the attackers came on they paused occasionally wherever a projection gave them sufficient foothold and launched arrows and spears at the defenders above them. During the entire battle both sides hurled taunts and insults at one another—the human beings naturally excelling the brutes in the coarseness and vileness of their vilification and invective.

The "firing-line" of the brute-men wielded no weapon other than their long fiber nooses. When a foeman came within range of them a noose would settle unerringly about him and he would be dragged, fighting and yelling, to the cliff-top, unless, as occasionally occurred, he was quick enough to draw his knife and cut the rope above him, in which event he usually plunged downward to a no less certain death than that which awaited him above.

Those who were hauled up within reach of the powerful clutches of the defenders had the nooses snatched from them and were catapulted back through the first line to the second, where they were seized and killed by the simple expedient of a single powerful closing of mighty fangs upon the backs of their necks.

But the arrows of the invaders were taking a much heavier toll than the nooses of the defenders and I foresaw that it was but a matter of time before Hooja's forces must conquer unless the brute-men changed their tactics, or the cave men tired of the battle.

Gr-gr-gr was standing in the center of the first line. All about him were boulders and large fragments of broken rock. I approached him and without a word toppled a large mass of rock over the edge of the cliff. It fell directly upon the head of an archer, crushing him to instant death and carrying his mangled corpse with it to the bottom of the declivity, and on its way brushing three more of the attackers into the hereafter.

Gr-gr-gr turned toward me in surprise. For an instant he appeared to doubt the sincerity of my motives. I felt that perhaps my time had come when he reached for me with one of his giant paws; but I dodged him, and running a few paces to the right hurled down another missile. It, too, did its allotted work of destruction. Then I picked up smaller fragments and with all the control and accuracy for which I had earned justly deserved fame in my collegiate days I rained down a hail of death upon those beneath me.

Gr-gr-gr was coming toward me again. I pointed to the litter of rubble upon the cliff-top.

"Hurl these down upon the enemy!" I cried to him. "Tell your warriors to throw rocks down upon them!"

At my words the others of the first line, who had been interested spectators of my tactics, seized upon great boulders or bits of rock, whichever came first to their hands, and, without waiting for a command from Gr-gr-gr, deluged the terrified cave men with a perfect avalanche of stone. In less than no time the cliff-face was stripped of enemies and the village of Gr-gr-gr was saved.

Gr-gr-gr was standing beside me when the last of the cave men disappeared in rapid flight down the valley. He was looking at me intently.

"Those were your people," he said. "Why did you kill them?"

"They were not my people," I returned. "I have told you that before, but you would not believe me. Will you believe me now when I tell you that I hate Hooja and his tribe as much as you do? Will you believe me when I tell you that I wish to be the friend of Gr-gr-gr?"

For some time he stood there beside me, scratching his head. Evidently it was no less difficult for him to readjust his preconceived conclusions than it is for most human beings; but finally the idea percolated—which it might never have done had he been a man, or I might qualify that statement by saying had he been some men. Finally he spoke.

"Gilak," he said, "you have made Gr-gr-gr ashamed. He would have killed you. How can he reward you?"

"Set me free," I replied quickly.

"You are free," he said. "You may go down when you wish, or you may stay with us. If you go you may always return. We are your friends."

Naturally, I elected to go. I explained all over again to Gr-gr-gr the nature of my mission. He listened attentively; after I had done he offered to send some of his people with me to guide me to Hooja's village. I was not slow in accepting his offer.

First, however, we must eat. The hunters upon whom Hooja's men had fallen had brought back the meat of a great thag. There would be a feast to commemorate the victory—a feast and dancing.

I had never witnessed a tribal function of the brute-folk, though I had often heard strange sounds coming from the village, where I had not been allowed since my capture. Now I took part in one of their orgies.

It will live forever in my memory. The combination of bestiality and humanity was oftentimes pathetic, and again grotesque or horrible. Beneath the glaring noonday sun, in the sweltering heat of the mesa-top, the huge, hairy creatures leaped in a great circle. They coiled and threw their fiber-ropes; they hurled taunts and insults at an imaginary foe; they fell upon the carcass of the thag and literally tore it to pieces; and they ceased only when, gorged, they could no longer move.

I had to wait until the processes of digestion had released my escort from its torpor. Some had eaten until their abdomens were so distended that I thought they must burst, for beside the thag there had been fully a hundred antelopes of various sizes and varied degrees of decomposition, which they had unearthed from burial beneath the floors of their lairs to grace the banquet-board.

But at last we were started—six great males and myself. Gr-gr-gr had returned my weapons to me, and at last I was once more upon my oft-interrupted way toward my goal. Whether I should find Dian at the end of my journey or no I could not even surmise; but I was none the less impatient to be off, for if only the worst lay in store for me I wished to know even the worst at once.

I could scarce believe that my proud mate would still be alive in the power of Hooja; but time upon Pellucidar is so strange a thing that I realized that to her or to him only a few minutes might have elapsed since his subtle trickery had enabled him to steal her away from Phutra. Or she might have found the means either to repel his advances or escape him.

As we descended the cliff we disturbed a great pack of large hyena-like beasts—*hyaena spelaeus,* Perry calls them—who were busy among the corpses of the cave men fallen in battle. The ugly creatures were far from the cowardly things that our own hyenas are reputed to be; they stood their ground with bared fangs as we approached them. But, as I was later to learn, so formidable are the brute-folk that there are few even of the larger carnivora that will not make way for them when they go abroad. So the hyenas moved a little from our line of march, closing in again upon their feasts when we had passed.

We made our way steadily down the rim of the beautiful river which flows the length of the island, coming at last to a wood rather denser than any that I had before encountered in this country. Well within this forest my escort halted.

"There!" they said, and pointed ahead. "We are to go no farther."

Thus having guided me to my destination they left me. Ahead of me, through the trees, I could see what appeared to be the foot of a steep hill. Toward this I made my way. The forest ran to the very base of a cliff, in the face of which were the mouths of many caves. They appeared untenanted; but I decided to watch for a while before venturing farther. A large tree, densely foliaged, offered a splendid vantage-point from which to spy upon the cliff, so I clambered among its branches where, securely hidden, I could watch what transpired about the caves.

It seemed that I had scarcely settled myself in a comfortable position before a party of cave men emerged from one of the smaller apertures in the cliff-face, about fifty feet from the base. They descended into the forest and disappeared. Soon after came several others from the same cave, and after them, at a short interval, a score of women and children, who came into the wood to gather fruit. There were several warriors with them—a guard, I presume.

After this came other parties, and two or three groups who passed out of the forest and up the cliff-face to enter the same cave. I could not understand it. All who had come out had emerged from the same cave. All who returned re-entered it. No other cave gave evidence of habitation, and no cave but one of extraordinary size could have accommodated all the people whom I had seen pass in and out of its mouth.

For a long time I sat and watched the coming and going of great numbers of the cave-folk. Not once did one leave the cliff by any other opening save that from which I had seen the first party come, nor did any re-enter the cliff through another aperture.

What a cave it must be, I thought, that houses an entire tribe! But, dissatisfied of the truth of my surmise, I climbed higher among the branches of the tree that I might get a better view of other portions of the cliff. High above the ground I reached a point whence I could see the summit of the hill. Evidently it was a flat-topped butte similar to that on which dwelt the tribe of Gr-gr-gr.

As I sat gazing at it a figure appeared at the very edge. It was that of a young girl in whose hair was a gorgeous bloom plucked from some flowering tree of the forest. I had seen her pass beneath me but a short while before and enter the small cave that had swallowed all of the returning tribesmen.

The mystery was solved. The cave was but the mouth of a passage that led upward through the cliff to the summit of the hill. It served merely as an avenue from their lofty citadel to the valley below.

No sooner had the truth flashed upon me than the realization came that I must seek some other means of reaching the village, for to pass unobserved through this well-traveled thoroughfare would be impossible. At the moment there was no one in sight below me, so I slid quickly from my arboreal watch-tower to the ground and moved rapidly away to the right with the intention of circling the hill if necessary until I had found an unwatched spot where I might have some slight chance of scaling the heights and reaching the top unseen.

I kept close to the edge of the forest, in the very midst of which the hill seemed to rise. Though I carefully scanned the cliff as I traversed its base, I saw no sign of any other entrance than that to which my guides had led me.

After some little time the roar of the sea broke upon my ears. Shortly after I came upon the broad ocean which breaks at this point at the very foot of the great hill where Hooja had found safe refuge for himself and his villains.

I was just about to clamber along the jagged rocks which lie at the base of the cliff next to the sea, in search of some foothold to the top, when I chanced to see a canoe rounding the end of the island. I threw myself down behind a large boulder where I could watch the dugout and its occupants without myself being seen.

They paddled toward me for a while and then, about a hundred yards from me, they turned straight in toward the foot of the frowning cliffs. From where I was it seemed that they were bent upon self-destruction, since the roar of the breakers beating upon the perpendicular rock-face appeared to offer only death to any one who might venture within their relentless clutch.

A mass of rock would soon hide them from my view; but so keen was the excitement of the instant that I could not refrain from crawling forward to a point whence I could watch the dashing of the small craft to pieces on the jagged rocks that loomed before her, although I risked discovery from above to accomplish my design.

When I had reached a point where I could again see the dugout, I was just in time to see it glide unharmed between two needle-pointed sentinels of granite and float quietly upon the unruffled bosom of a tiny cove.

Again I crouched behind a boulder to observe what would next transpire; nor did I have long to wait. The dugout, which contained but two men, was drawn close to the rocky wall. A fiber rope, one end of which was tied to the boat, was made fast about a projection of the cliff face.

Then the two men commenced the ascent of the almost perpendicular wall toward the summit several hundred feet above. I looked on in amazement, for, splendid climbers though the cave men of Pellucidar are, I never before had seen so remarkable a feat performed. Upward they moved without a pause, to disappear at last over the summit.

When I felt reasonably sure that they had gone for a while at least I crawled from my hiding-place and at the risk of a broken neck leaped and scrambled to the spot where their canoe was moored.

If they had scaled that cliff I could, and if I couldn't I should die in the attempt.

But when I turned to the accomplishment of the task I found it easier than I had imagined it would be, since I immediately discovered that shallow hand- and footholds had been scooped in the cliff's rocky face, forming a crude ladder from the base to the summit.

At last I reached the top, and very glad I was, too. Cautiously I raised my head until my eyes were above the cliff-crest. Before me spread a rough mesa, liberally sprinkled with large boulders. There was no village in sight nor any living creature.

I drew myself to level ground and stood erect. A few trees grew among the boulders. Very carefully I advanced from tree to tree and boulder to boulder toward the inland end of the mesa. I stopped often to listen and look cautiously about me in every direction.

How I wished that I had my revolvers and rifle! I would not have to worm my way like a scared cat toward Hooja's village, nor did I relish doing so now; but Dian's life might hinge upon the success of my venture, and so I could not afford to take chances. To have met suddenly with discovery and had a score or more of armed warriors upon me might have been very grand and heroic; but it would have immediately put an end to all my earthly activities, nor have accomplished aught in the service of Dian.

Well, I must have traveled nearly a mile across that mesa without seeing a sign of anyone, when all of a sudden, as I crept around the edge of a boulder, I ran plump into a man, down on all fours like myself, crawling toward me.

CHAPTER X

THE RAID ON THE CAVE-PRISON

HIS head was turned over his shoulder as I first saw him—he was looking back toward the village. As I leaped for him his eyes fell upon me. Never in my life have I seen a more surprised mortal than this poor cave man. Before he could utter a single scream of warning or alarm I had my fingers on his throat and had dragged him behind the boulder, where I proceeded to sit upon him, while I figured out what I had best do with him.

He struggled a little at first, but finally lay still, and so I released the pressure of my fingers at his windpipe, for which I imagine he was quite thankful—I know that I should have been.

I hated to kill him in cold blood; but what else I was to do with him I could not see, for to turn him loose would have been merely to have the entire village aroused and down upon me in a moment. The fellow lay looking up at me with the surprise still deeply written on his countenance. At last, all of a sudden, a look of recognition entered his eyes.

"I have seen you before," he said. "I saw you in the arena at the Mahars' city of Phutra when the thipdars dragged the tarag from you and your mate. I never understood that. Afterward they put me in the arena with two warriors from Gombul."

He smiled in recollection.

"It would have been the same had there been ten warriors from Gombul. I slew them, winning my freedom. Look!"

He half turned his left shoulder toward me, exhibiting the newly healed scar of the Mahars' branded mark.

"Then," he continued, "as I was returning to my people I met some of them fleeing. They told me that one called Hooja the Sly One had come and seized our village, putting our people into slavery. So I hurried hither to learn the truth, and, sure enough, here I found Hooja and his wicked men living in my village, and my father's people but slaves among them.

"I was discovered and captured, but Hooja did not kill me. I am the chief's son, and through me he hoped to win my father's warriors back to the village to help him in a great war he says that he will soon commence.

"Among his prisoners is Dian the Beautiful One, whose brother, Dacor the Strong One, chief of Amoz, once saved my life when he came to Thuria to steal a mate. I helped him capture her, and we are good friends. So when I learned that Dian the Beautiful One was Hooja's prisoner, I told him that I would not aid him if he harmed her.

"Recently one of Hooja's warriors overheard me talking with another prisoner. We were planning to combine all the prisoners, seize weapons, and when most of Hooja's warriors were away, slay the rest and retake our hilltop. Had we done so we could have held it, for there are only two entrances—the narrow tunnel at one end and the steep path up the cliffs at the other.

"But when Hooja heard what we had planned he was very angry, and ordered that I die. They bound me hand and foot and placed me in a cave until all the warriors should return to witness my death; but while they were away I heard someone calling me in a muffled voice which seemed to come from the wall of the cave. When I replied the voice, which was a woman's, told me that she had overheard all that had passed between me and those who had brought me thither, and that she was Dacor's sister and would find a way to help me.

"Presently a little hole appeared in the wall at the point from which the voice had come. After a time I saw a woman's hand digging with a bit of stone. Dacor's sister made a hole in the wall between the cave where I lay bound and that in which she had been confined, and soon she was by my side and had cut my bonds.

"We talked then, and I offered to make the attempt to take her away and back to the land of Sari, where she told me she would be able to learn the whereabouts of her mate. Just now I was going to the other end of the island to see if a boat lay there, and if the way was clear for our escape. Most of the boats are always away now, for a great many of Hooja's men and nearly all the slaves are upon the Island of Trees, where Hooja is having many boats built to carry his warriors across the water to the mouth of a great river which he discovered while he was returning from Phutra—a vast river that empties into the sea there."

The speaker pointed toward the northeast.

"It is wide and smooth and slow-running almost to the land of Sari," he added.

"And where is Dian the Beautiful One now?" I asked.

I had released my prisoner as soon as I found that he was Hooja's enemy, and now the pair of us were squatting beside the boulder while he told his story.

"She returned to the cave where she had been imprisoned," he replied, "and is awaiting me there."

"There is no danger that Hooja will come while you are away?"

"Hooja is upon the Island of Trees," he replied.

"Can you direct me to the cave so that I can find it alone?" I asked.

He said he could, and in the strange yet explicit fashion of the Pellucidarians he explained minutely how I might reach the cave where he had been imprisoned, and through the hole in its wall reach Dian.

I thought it best for but one of us to return, since two could accomplish but little more than one and would double the risk of discovery. In the meantime he could make his way to the sea and guard the boat, which I told him lay there at the foot of the cliff.

I told him to await us at the cliff-top, and if Dian came alone to do his best to get away with her and take her to Sari, as I thought it quite possible that, in case of detection and pursuit, it might be necessary for me to hold off Hooja's people while Dian made her way alone to where my new friend was to await her. I impressed upon him the fact that he might have to resort to trickery or even to force to get Dian to leave me; but I made him promise that he would sacrifice everything, even his life, in an attempt to rescue Dacor's sister.

Then we parted—he to take up his position where he could watch the boat and await Dian, I to crawl cautiously on toward the caves. I had no difficulty in following the directions given me by Juag, the name by which Dacor's friend said he was called.

There was the leaning tree, my first point he told me to look for after rounding the boulder where we had met. After that I crawled to the balanced rock, a huge boulder resting upon a tiny base no larger than the palm of your hand.

From here I had my first view of the village of caves. A low bluff ran diagonally across one end of the mesa, and in the face of this bluff were the mouths of many caves. Zig-zag trails led up to them, and narrow ledges scooped from the face of the soft rock connected those upon the same level.

The cave in which Juag had been confined was at the extreme end of the cliff nearest me. By taking advantage of the bluff itself, I could approach within a few feet of the aperture without being visible from any other cave. There were few people about at the time; most of these were congregated at the foot of the far end of the bluff, where they were so engrossed in excited conversation that I felt but little fear of detection. However I exercised the greatest care in approaching the cliff. After watching for a while until I caught an instant when every head was turned away from me, I darted, rabbitlike, into the cave.

Like many of the man-made caves of Pellucidar, this one consisted of three chambers, one behind another, and all unlit except for what sunlight filtered in through the external opening. The result was gradually increasing darkness as one passed into each succeeding chamber.

In the last of the three I could just distinguish objects, and that was all. As I was groping around the walls for the hole that should lead into the cave where Dian was imprisoned, I heard a man's voice quite close to me.

The speaker had evidently but just entered, for he spoke in a loud tone, demanding the whereabouts of one whom he had come in search of.

"Where are you, woman?" he cried. "Hooja has sent for you."

And then a woman's voice answered him: "And what does Hooja want of me?"

The voice was Dian's. I groped in the direction of the sounds, feeling for the hole.

"He wishes you brought to the Island of Trees," replied the man; "for he is ready to take you as his mate."

"I will not go," said Dian. "I will die first."

"I am sent to bring you, and bring you I shall."

I could hear him crossing the cave toward her.

Frantically I clawed the wall of the cave in which I was in an effort to find the elusive aperture that would lead me to Dian's side.

I heard the sound of a scuffle in the next cave. Then my fingers sank into loose rock and earth in the side of the cave. In an instant I realized why I had been unable to find the opening while I had been lightly feeling the surface of the walls—Dian had blocked up the hole she had made lest it arouse suspicion and lead to an early discovery of Juag's escape.

Plunging my weight against the crumbling mass, I sent it crashing into the adjoining cavern. With it came I, David, Emperor of Pellucidar. I doubt if any other potentate in a world's history ever made a more undignified entrance. I landed head first on all fours, but I came to quickly and was on my feet before the man in the dark guessed what had happened.

He saw me, though, when I arose and, sensing that no friend came thus precipitately, turned to meet me even as I charged him. I had my stone knife in my hand, and he had his. In the darkness of the cave there was little opportunity for a display of science, though even at that I venture to say that we fought a very pretty duel.

Before I came to Pellucidar I do not recall that I ever had seen a stone knife, and I am sure that I never fought with a knife of any description; but now I do not have to take my hat off to any of them when it comes to wielding that primitive yet wicked weapon.

I could just see Dian in the darkness, but I knew that she could not see my features or recognize me; and I enjoyed in anticipation, even while I was fighting for her life and mine, her dear joy when she should discover that it was I who was her deliverer.

My opponent was large, but he also was active and no mean knife-man. He caught me once fairly in the shoulder—I carry the scar yet, and shall carry it to the grave. And then he did a foolish thing, for as I leaped back to gain a second in which to calm the shock of the wound he rushed after me and tried to clinch. He rather neglected his knife for the moment in his greater desire to get his hands on me. Seeing the opening, I swung my left fist fairly to the point of his jaw.

Down he went. Before ever he could scramble up again I was on him and had buried my knife in his heart. Then I stood up—and there was Dian facing me and peering at me through the dense gloom.

"You are not Juag!" she exclaimed. "Who are you?"

I took a step toward her, my arms outstretched.

"It is I, Dian," I said. "It is David."

At the sound of my voice she gave a little cry in which tears were mingled—a pathetic little cry that told me all without words how far hope had gone from her—and then she ran forward and threw herself in my arms. I covered her perfect lips and her beautiful face with kisses, and stroked her thick black hair, and told her again and again what she already knew—what she had known for years—that I loved her better than all else which two worlds had to offer. We couldn't devote much time, though, to the happiness of love-making, for we were in the midst of enemies who might discover us at any moment.

I drew her into the adjoining cave. Thence we made our way to the mouth of the cave that had given me entrance to the cliff. Here I reconnoitered for a moment, and seeing the coast clear, ran swiftly forth with Dian at my side. We dodged around the cliff-end, then paused for an instant, listening. No sound reached our ears to indicate that any had seen us, and we moved cautiously onward along the way by which I had come.

As we went Dian told me that her captors had informed her how close I had come in search of her—even to the Land of Awful Shadow—and how one of Hooja's men who knew me had discovered me asleep and robbed me of all my possessions. And then how Hooja had sent four others to find me and take me prisoner. But these men, she said, had not yet returned, or at least she had not heard of their return.

"Nor will you ever," I responded, "for they have gone to that place whence none ever returns." I then related my adventure with these four.

We had come almost to the cliff-edge where Juag should be awaiting us when we saw two men walking rapidly toward the same spot from another direction. They did not see us, nor did they see Juag, whom I now discovered hiding behind a low bush close to the verge of the precipice which drops into the sea at this point. As quickly as possible, without exposing ourselves too much to the enemy, we hastened forward that we might reach Juag as quickly as they.

But they noticed him first and immediately charged him, for one of them had been his guard, and they had both been sent to search for him, his escape having been discovered between the time he left the cave and the time when I reached it. Evidently they had wasted precious moments looking for him in other portions of the mesa.

When I saw that the two of them were rushing him, I called

out to attract their attention to the fact that they had more than a single man to cope with. They paused at the sound of my voice and looked about.

When they discovered Dian and me they exchanged a few words, and one of them continued toward Juag while the other turned upon us. As he came nearer I saw that he carried in his hand one of my six-shooters, but he was holding it by the barrel, evidently mistaking it for some sort of war-club or tomahawk.

I could scarce refrain a grin when I thought of the wasted possibilities of that deadly revolver in the hands of an untutored warrior of the stone age. Had he but reversed it and pulled the trigger he might still be alive; maybe he is for all I know, since I did not kill him then. When he was about twenty feet from me I flung my javelin with a quick movement that I had learned from Ghak. He ducked to avoid it, and instead of receiving it in his heart, for which it was intended, he got it on the side of the head.

Down he went all in a heap. Then I glanced toward Juag. He was having a most exciting time. The fellow pitted against Juag was a veritable giant; he was hacking and hewing away at the poor slave with a villainous-looking knife that might have been designed for butchering mastodons. Step by step, he was forcing Juag back toward the edge of the cliff with a fiendish cunning that permitted his adversary no chance to side-step the terrible consequences of retreat in this direction. I saw quickly that in another moment Juag must deliberately hurl himself to death over the precipice or be pushed over by his foeman.

And as I saw Juag's predicament I saw, too, in the same instant, a way to relieve him. Leaping quickly to the side of the fellow I had just felled, I snatched up my fallen revolver. It was a desperate chance to take, and I realized it in the instant that I threw the gun up from my hip and pulled the trigger. There was no time to aim. Juag was upon the very brink of the chasm. His relentless foe was pushing him hard, beating at him furiously with the heavy knife.

And then the revolver spoke—loud and sharp. The giant threw his hands above his head, whirled about like a huge top, and lunged forward over the precipice.

And Juag?

He cast a single affrighted glance in my direction—never before, of course, had he heard the report of a firearm—and with a howl of dismay he, too, turned and plunged headforemost from sight. Horror-struck, I hastened to the brink of the abyss just in time to see two splashes upon the surface of the little cove below.

For an instant I stood there watching with Dian at my side. Then, to my utter amazement, I saw Juag rise to the surface and swim strongly toward the boat.

The fellow had dived that incredible distance and come up unharmed!

I called to him to await us below, assuring him that he need have no fear of my weapon, since it would harm only my enemies. He shook his head and muttered something which I could not hear at so great a distance; but when I pushed him he promised to wait for us. At the same instant Dian caught my arm and pointed toward the village. My shot had brought a crowd of natives on the run toward us.

The fellow whom I had stunned with my javelin had regained consciousness and scrambled to his feet. He was now racing as fast as he could go back toward his people. It looked mighty dark for Dian and me with that ghastly descent between us and even the beginnings of liberty, and a horde of savage enemies advancing at a rapid run.

There was but one hope. That was to get Dian started for the bottom without delay. I took her in my arms just for an instant— I felt, somehow, that it might be for the last time. For the life of me I couldn't see how both of us could escape.

I asked her if she could make the descent alone—if she were not afraid. She smiled up at me bravely and shrugged her shoulders. She afraid! So beautiful is she that I am always having difficulty in remembering that she is a primitive, half-savage cave girl of the stone age, and often find myself mentally limiting her capacities to those of the effete and overcivilized beauties of the outer crust.

"And you?" she asked as she swung over the edge of the cliff.

"I shall follow you after I take a shot or two at our friends," I replied. "I just want to give them a taste of this new medicine which is going to cure Pellucidar of all its ills. That will stop them long enough for me to join you. Now hurry, and tell Juag to be ready to shove off the moment I reach the boat, or the instant that it becomes apparent that I cannot reach it.

"You, Dian, must return to Sari if anything happens to me, that you may devote your life to carrying out with Perry the hopes and plans for Pellucidar that are so dear to my heart. Promise me, dear."

She hated to promise to desert me, nor would she, only shaking her head and making no move to descend. The tribesmen were nearing us. Juag was shouting up to us from below. It was evident that he realized from my actions that I was attempting to persuade

Dian to descend, and that grave danger threatened us from above
  "Dive!" he cried. "Dive!"

I looked at Dian and then down at the abyss below us. The cove
appeared no larger than a saucer. How Juag ever had hit it I could
not guess.

  "Dive!" cried Juag. "It is the only way—there is no time to
climb down."

CHAPTER XI

ESCAPE

DIAN glanced downward and shuddered. Her tribe were hill people—they were not accustomed to swimming other than in quiet
rivers and placid lakelets. It was not the steep that appalled her.
It was the ocean—vast, mysterious, terrible.

To dive into it from this great height was beyond her. I couldn't
wonder, either. To have attempted it myself seemed too preposterous even for thought. Only one consideration could have
prompted me to leap headforemost from that giddy height—suicide; or at least so I thought at the moment.

  "Quick!" I urged Dian. "You cannot dive; but I can hold them
until you reach safety."

  "And you?" she asked once more. "Can you dive when they come
too close? Otherwise you could not escape them if you waited here
until I reached the bottom."

I saw that she would not leave me unless she thought that I could
make that frightful dive as we had seen Juag make it. I glanced
once downward; then with a mental shrug I assured her that I
would dive the moment that she reached the boat. Satisfied, she
began the descent carefully, yet swiftly. I watched her for a moment, my heart in my mouth lest some slight misstep or the slip-
ping of a finger-hold should pitch her to a frightful death upon
the rocks below.

Then I turned toward the advancing Hoojans—"Hoosiers,"
Perry dubbed them—even going so far as to christen this island
where Hooja held sway Indiana; it is so marked now upon our
maps. They were coming on at a great rate. I raised my revolver,
took deliberate aim at the foremost warrior, and pulled the trig-

ger. With the bark of the gun the fellow lunged forward. His
head doubled beneath him. He rolled over and over two or three
times before he came to a stop, to lie very quietly in the thick
grass among the brilliant wild flowers.

Those behind him halted. One of them hurled a javelin toward
me, but it fell short—they were just beyond javelin-range. There
were two armed with bows and arrows; these I kept my eyes on.
All of them appeared awe-struck and frightened by the sound and
effect of the firearm. They kept looking from the corpse to me
and jabbering among themselves.

I took advantage of the lull in hostilities to throw a quick glance
over the edge toward Dian. She was half-way down the cliff and
progressing finely. Then I turned back toward the enemy. One
of the bowmen was fitting an arrow to his bow. I raised my hand.

"Stop!" I cried. "Whoever shoots at me or advances toward me
I shall kill as I killed him!"

I pointed at the dead man. The fellow lowered his bow. Again
there was animated discussion. I could see that those who were
not armed with bows were urging something upon the two who
were.

At last the majority appeared to prevail, for simultaneously the
two archers raised their weapons. At the same instant I fired at
one of them, dropping him in his tracks. The other, however,
launched his missile, but the report of my gun had given him
such a start that the arrow flew wild above my head. A second
after and he, too, was sprawled upon the sward with a round hole
between his eyes. It had been a rather good shot.

I glanced over the edge again. Dian was almost at the bottom.
I could see Juag standing just beneath her with his hands up-
stretched to assist her.

A sullen roar from the warriors recalled my attention toward
them. They stood shaking their fists at me and yelling insults.
From the direction of the village I saw a single warrior coming
to join them. He was a huge fellow, and when he strode among
them I could tell by his bearing and their deference toward him
that he was a chieftain. He listened to all they had to tell of the
happenings of the last few minutes; then with a command and
a roar he started for me with the whole pack at his heels. All they
had needed had arrived—namely, a brave leader.

I had two unfired cartridges in the chambers of my gun. I let
the big warrior have one of them, thinking that his death would
stop them all. But I guess they were worked up to such a frenzy
of rage by this time that nothing would have stopped them. At

any rate, they only yelled the louder as he fell and increased their speed toward me. I dropped another with my remaining cartridge.

Then they were upon me—or almost. I thought of my promise to Dian—the awful abyss was behind me—a big devil with a huge bludgeon in front of me. I grasped my six-shooter by the barrel and hurled it squarely in his face with all my strength.

Then, without waiting to learn the effect of my throw, I wheeled, ran the few steps to the edge, and leaped as far out over that frightful chasm as I could. I know something of diving, and all that I know I put into that dive, which I was positive would be my last.

For a couple of hundred feet I fell in a horizontal position. The momentum I gained was terrific. I could feel the air almost as a solid body, so swiftly I hurtled through it. Then my position gradually changed to the vertical, and with hands outstretched I slipped through the air, cleaving it like a flying arrow. Just before I struck the water a perfect shower of javelins fell all about. My enemies had rushed to the brink and hurled their weapons after me. By a miracle I was untouched.

In the final instant I saw that I had cleared the rocks and was going to strike the water fairly. Then I was in and plumbing the depths. I suppose I didn't really go very far down, but it seemed to me that I should never stop. When at last I dared curve my hands upward and divert my progress toward the surface, I thought that I should explode for air before I ever saw the sun again except through a swirl of water. But at last my head popped above the waves, and I filled my lungs with air.

Before me was the boat, from which Juag and Dian were clambering. I couldn't understand why they were deserting it now, when we were about to set out for the mainland in it; but when I reached its side I understood. Two heavy javelins, missing Dian and Juag by but a hair's breadth, had sunk deep into the bottom of the dugout in a straight line with the grain of the wood, and split her almost in two from stem to stern. She was useless.

Juag was leaning over a near-by rock, his hand outstretched to aid me in clambering to his side; nor did I lose any time in availing myself of his proffered assistance. An occasional javelin was still dropping perilously close to us, so we hastened to draw as close as possible to the cliffside, where we were comparatively safe from the missiles.

Here we held a brief conference, in which it was decided that our only hope now lay in making for the opposite end of the island as quickly as we could, and utilizing the boat that I had hidden there to continue our journey to the mainland.

Gathering up three of the least damaged javelins that had fallen about us, we set out upon our journey, keeping well toward the south side of the island, which Juag said was less frequented by the Hoojans than the central portion where the river ran. I think that this ruse must have thrown our pursuers off our track, since we saw nothing of them nor heard any sound of pursuit during the greater portion of our march the length of the island.

But the way Juag had chosen was rough and roundabout, so that we consumed one or two more marches in covering the distance than if we had followed the river. This it was which proved our undoing.

Those who sought us must have sent a party up the river immediately after we escaped; for when we came at last onto the river-trail not far from our destination, there can be no doubt but that we were seen by Hoojans who were just ahead of us on the stream. The result was that as we were passing through a clump of bush a score of warriors leaped out upon us, and before we could scarce strike a blow in defense, had disarmed and bound us.

For a time thereafter I seemed to be entirely bereft of hope. I could see no ray of promise in the future—only immediate death for Juag and me, which didn't concern me much in the face of what lay in store for Dian.

Poor child! What an awful life she had led! From the moment that I had first seen her chained in the slave caravan of the Mahars until now, a prisoner of a no less cruel creature, I could recall but a few brief intervals of peace and quiet in her tempestuous existence. Before I had known her, Jubal the Ugly One had pursued her across a savage world to make her his mate. She had eluded him, and finally I had slain him; but terror and privations, and exposure to fierce beasts had haunted her footsteps during all her lonely flight from him. And when I had returned to the outer world the old trials had recommenced with Hooja in Jubal's rôle. I could almost have wished for death to vouchsafe her that peace which fate seemed to deny her in this life.

I spoke to her on the subject, suggesting that we expire together.

"Do not fear, David," she replied. "I shall end my life before ever Hooja can harm me; but first I shall see that Hooja dies."

She drew from her breast a little leathern thong, to the end of which was fastened a tiny pouch.

"What have you there?" I asked.

"Do you recall that time you stepped upon the thing you call viper in your world?" she asked.

I nodded.

"The accident gave you the idea for the poisoned arrows with which we fitted the warriors of the empire," she continued. "And, too, it gave me an idea. For a long time I have carried a viper's fang in my bosom. It has given me strength to endure many dangers, for it has always assured me immunity from the ultimate insult. I am not ready to die yet. First let Hooja embrace the viper's fang."

So we did not die together, and I am glad now that we did not. It is always a foolish thing to contemplate suicide; for no matter how dark the future may appear today, tomorrow may hold for us that which will alter our whole life in an instant, revealing to us nothing but sunshine and happiness. So, for my part, I shall always wait for tomorrow.

In Pellucidar, where it is always today, the wait may not be so long, and so it proved for us. As we were passing a lofty, flat-topped hill through a parklike wood a perfect network of fiber ropes fell suddenly about our guard, enmeshing them. A moment later a horde of our friends, the hairy gorilla-men with the mild eyes and long faces of sheep, leaped among them.

It was a very interesting fight. I was sorry that my bonds prevented me from taking part in it, but I urged on the brute-men with my voice, and cheered old Gr-gr-gr, their chief, each time that his mighty jaws crunched out the life of a Hoojan. When the battle was over we found that a few of our captors had escaped, but the majority of them lay dead about us. The gorilla-men paid no further attention to them. Gr-gr-gr turned to me.

"Gr-gr-gr and all his people are your friends," he said. "One saw the warriors of the Sly One and followed them. He saw them capture you, and then he flew to the village as fast as he could go and told me all that he had seen. The rest you know. You did much for Gr-gr-gr and Gr-gr-gr's people. We shall always do much for you."

I thanked him; and when I had told him of our escape and our destination, he insisted on accompanying us to the sea with a great number of his fierce males. Nor were we at all loath to accept his escort. We found the canoe where I had hidden it, and bidding Gr-gr-gr and his warriors farewell, the three of us embarked for the mainland.

I questioned Juag upon the feasibility of attempting to cross to the mouth of the great river of which he had told me, and up which he said we might paddle almost to Sari; but he urged me not to attempt it, since we had but a single paddle and no water or food. I had to admit the wisdom of his advice, but the desire to

explore this great waterway was strong upon me, arousing in me
at last a determination to make the attempt after first gaining the
mainland and rectifying our deficiencies.

We landed several miles north of Thuria in a little cove that
seemed to offer protection from the heavier seas which sometimes
run, even upon these usually pacific oceans of Pellucidar. Here I
outlined to Dian and Juag the plans I had in mind. They were
to fit the canoe with a small sail, the purposes of which I had to
explain to them both—since neither had ever seen or heard of
such a contrivance before. Then they were to hunt for food which
we could transport with us, and prepare a receptacle for water.

These two latter items were more in Juag's line, but he kept
muttering about the sail and the wind for a long time. I could
see that he was not even half convinced that any such ridiculous
contraption could make a canoe move through the water.

We hunted near the coast for a while, but were not rewarded
with any particular luck. Finally we decided to hide the canoe and
strike inland in search of game. At Juag's suggestion we dug a hole
in the sand at the upper edge of the beach and buried the craft,
smoothing the surface over nicely and throwing aside the excess
material we had excavated. Then we set out away from the sea.
Traveling in Thuria is less arduous than under the midday sun
which perpetually glares down on the rest of Pellucidar's surface;
but it has its drawbacks, one of which is the depressing influence
exerted by the everlasting shade of the Land of Awful Shadow.

The farther inland we went the darker it became, until we were
moving at last through an endless twilight. The vegetation here
was sparse and of a weird, colorless nature, though what did grow
was wondrous in shape and form. Often we saw huge lidi, or beasts
of burden, striding across the dim landscape, browsing upon the
grotesque vegetation or drinking from the slow and sullen rivers
that run down from the Lidi Plains to empty into the sea in
Thuria.

What we sought was either thag—a sort of gigantic elk—or one
of the larger species of antelope, the flesh of either of which dries
nicely in the sun. The bladder of the thag would make a fine water-
bottle, and its skin, I figured, would be a good sail. We traveled
a considerable distance inland, entirely crossing the Land of Awful Shadow and emerging at last upon that portion of the Lidi
Plains which lies in the pleasant sunlight. Above us the pendent
world revolved upon its axis, filling me especially—and Dian to
an almost equal state—with wonder and insatiable curiosity as
to what strange forms of life existed among the hills and valleys

and along the seas and rivers, which we could plainly see.

Before us stretched the horizonless expanses of vast Pellucidar, the Lidi Plains rolling up about us, while hanging high in the heavens to the northwest of us I thought I discerned the many towers which marked the entrances to the distant Mahar city, whose inhabitants preyed upon the Thurians.

Juag suggested that we travel to the northeast, where, he said, upon the verge of the plain we would find a wooded country in which game should be plentiful. Acting upon his advice, we came at last to a forest-jungle, through which wound innumerable game-paths. In the depths of this forbidding wood we came upon the fresh spoor of thag.

Shortly after, by careful stalking, we came within javelin-range of a small herd. Selecting a great bull, Juag and I hurled our weapons simultaneously, Dian reserving hers for an emergency. The beast staggered to his feet, bellowing. The rest of the herd was up and away in an instant, only the wounded bull remaining, with lowered head and roving eyes searching for the foe.

Then Juag exposed himself to the view of the bull—it is a part of the tactics of the hunt—while I stepped to one side behind a bush. The moment that the savage beast saw Juag he charged him. Juag ran straight away, that the bull might be lured past my hiding-place. On he came—tons of mighty bestial strength and rage.

Dian had slipped behind me. She, too, could fight a thag should emergency require. Ah, such a girl! A rightful empress of a stone age by every standard which two worlds might bring to measure her!

Crashing down toward us came the bull thag, bellowing and snorting, with the power of a hundred outer-earthly bulls. When he was opposite me I sprang for the heavy mane that covered his huge neck. To tangle my fingers in it was the work of but an instant. Then I was running along at the beast's shoulder.

Now, the theory upon which this hunting custom is based is one long ago discovered by experience, and that is that a thag cannot be turned from his charge once he has started toward the object of his wrath, so long as he can still see the thing he charges. He evidently believes that the man clinging to his mane is attempting to restrain him from overtaking his prey, and so he pays no attention to this enemy, who, of course, does not retard the mighty charge in the least.

Once in the gait of the plunging bull, it was but a slight matter to vault to his back, as cavalrymen mount their chargers upon the run. Juag was still running in plain sight ahead of the bull. His speed was but a trifle less than that of the monster that pursued him. These Pellucidarians are almost as fleet as deer; because I am not is one reason that I am always chosen for the close-in work of the thag-hunt. I could not keep in front of a charging thag long enough to give the killer time to do his work. I learned that the first—and last—time I tried it.

Once astride the bull's neck, I drew my long stone knife and, setting the point carefully over the brute's spine, drove it home with both hands. At the same instant I leaped clear of the stumbling animal. Now, no vertebrate can progress far with a knife through his spine, and the thag is no exception to the rule.

The fellow was down instantly. As he wallowed Juag returned, and the two of us leaped in when an opening afforded the opportunity and snatched our javelins from his side. Then we danced about him, more like two savages than anything else, until we got the opening we were looking for, when simultaneously, our javelins pierced his wild heart, stilling it forever.

The thag had covered considerable ground from the point at which I had leaped upon him. When, after despatching him, I looked back for Dian, I could see nothing of her. I called aloud, but receiving no reply, set out at a brisk trot to where I had left her. I had no difficulty in finding the self-same bush behind which we had hidden, but Dian was not there. Again and gain I called, to be rewarded only by silence. Where could she be? What could have become of her in the brief interval since I had seen her standing just behind me?

CHAPTER XII

KIDNAPED!

I SEARCHED about the spot carefully. At last I was rewarded by the discovery of her javelin, a few yards from the bush that had concealed us from the charging thag—her javelin and the indications of a struggle revealed by the trampled vegetation and the overlapping footprints of a woman and a man. Filled with consternation and dismay, I followed these latter to where they suddenly disappeared a hundred yards from where the struggle had occurred. There I saw the huge imprints of a lidi's feet.

With a hideous roar the beast turned and slunk toward the girl.

I drew my long knife and drove it home with both hands.

The story of the tragedy was all too plain. A Thurian had either been following us, or had accidentally espied Dian and taken a fancy to her. While Juag and I had been engaged with the thag, he had abducted her. I ran swiftly back to where Juag was working over the kill. As I approached him I saw that something was wrong in this quarter as well, for the islander was standing upon the carcass of the thag, his javelin poised for a throw.

When I had come nearer I saw the cause of his belligerent attitude. Just beyond him stood two large jaloks, or wolf-dogs, regarding him intently—a male and a female. Their behavior was rather peculiar, for they did not seem preparing to charge him. Rather, they were contemplating him in an attitude of questioning.

Juag heard me coming and turned toward me with a grin. These fellows love excitement. I could see by his expression that he was enjoying in anticipation the battle that seemed imminent. But he never hurled his javelin. A shout of warning from me stopped him, for I had seen the remnants of a rope dangling from the neck of the male jalok.

Juag again turned toward me, but this time in surprise. I was abreast him in a moment and, passing him, walked straight toward the two beasts. As I did so the female crouched with bared fangs. The male, however, leaped forward to meet me, not in deadly charge, but with every expression of delight and joy which the poor animal could exhibit.

It was Raja—the jalok whose life I had saved, and whom I then had tamed! There was no doubt that he was glad to see me. I now think that his seeming desertion of me had been but due to a desire to search out his ferocious mate and bring her, too, to live with me.

When Juag saw me fondling the great beast he was filled with consternation, but I did not have much time to spare to Raja while my mind was filled with the grief of my new loss. I was glad to see the brute, and I lost no time in taking him to Juag and making him understand that Juag, too, was to be Raja's friend. With the female the matter was more difficult, but Raja helped us out by growling savagely at her whenever she bared her fangs against us.

I told Juag of the disappearance of Dian, and of my suspicions as to the explanation of the catastrophe. He wanted to start right out after her, but I suggested that with Raja to help me it might be as well were he to remain and skin the thag, remove its bladder, and then return to where we had hidden the canoe on the beach. And so it was arranged that he was to do this and await me there for a reasonable time. I pointed to a great lake upon the surface of the pendent world above us, telling him that if after this lake had appeared four times I had not returned to go either by water or land to Sari and fetch Ghak with an army. Then, calling Raja after me, I set out after Dian and her abductor. First I took the wolf-dog to the spot where the man had fought with Dian. A few paces behind us followed Raja's fierce mate. I pointed to the ground where the evidences of the struggle were plainest and where the scent must have been strong to Raja's nostrils.

Then I grasped the remnant of leash that hung about his neck and urged him forward upon the trail. He seemed to understand. With nose to ground he set out upon his task. Dragging me after him, he trotted straight out upon the Lidi Plains, turning his steps in the direction of the Thurian village. I could have guessed as much!

Behind us trailed the female. After a while she closed upon us, until she ran quite close to me and at Raja's side. It was not long before she seemed as easy in my company as did her lord and master.

We must have covered considerable distance at a very rapid pace, for we had re-entered the great shadow, when we saw a huge lidi ahead of us, moving leisurely across the level plain. Upon its back were two human figures. If I could have known that the jaloks would not harm Dian I might have turned them loose upon the lidi and its master; but I could not know, and so dared take no chances.

However, the matter was taken out of my hands presently when Raja raised his head and caught sight of his quarry. With a lunge that hurled me flat and jerked the leash from my hand, he was gone with the speed of the wind after the giant lidi and its riders. At his side raced his shaggy mate, only a trifle smaller than he and no whit less savage.

They did not give tongue until the lidi itself discovered them and broke into a lumbering, awkward, but none the less rapid gallop. Then the two hound-beasts commenced to bay, starting with a low, plaintive note that rose, weird and hideous, to terminate in a series of short, sharp yelps. I feared that it might be the hunting-call of the pack; and if this were true, there would be slight chance for either Dian or her abductor—or myself, either, as far as that was concerned. So I redoubled my efforts to keep pace with the hunt; but I might as well have attempted to distance the bird upon the wing; as I have often reminded you, I am no runner. In that instance it was just as well that I am not, for my very slowness of foot played into my hands; while had I been fleeter, I might have lost Dian that time forever.

The lidi, with the hounds running close on either side, had almost disappeared in the darkness that enveloped the surrounding landscape, when I noted that it was bearing toward the right. This was accounted for by the fact that Raja ran upon his left side, and unlike his mate, kept leaping for the great beast's shoulder. The man on the lidi's back was prodding at the hyaenodon with his long spear, but still Raja kept springing up and snapping.

The effect of this was to turn the lidi toward the right, and the longer I watched the procedure the more convinced I became that Raja and his mate were working together with some end in view, for the she-dog merely galloped steadily at the lidi's right about opposite his rump.

I had seen jaloks hunting in packs, and I recalled now what for the time I had not thought of—the several that ran ahead and turned the quarry back toward the main body. This was precisely what Raja and his mate were doing—they were turning the lidi back toward me, or at least Raja was. Just why the female was keeping out of it I did not understand, unless it was that she was not entirely clear in her own mind as to precisely what her mate was attempting.

At any rate, I was sufficiently convinced to stop where I was and await developments, for I could readily realize two things. One was that I could never overhaul them before the damage was done if they should pull the lidi down now. The other thing was that if they did not pull it down for a few minutes it would have completed its circle and returned close to where I stood.

And this is just what happened. The lot of them were almost swallowed up in the twilight for a moment. Then they reappeared again, but this time far to the right and circling back in my general direction. I waited until I could get some clear idea of the right spot to gain that I might intercept the lidi; but even as I waited I saw the beast attempt to turn still more to the right— a move that would have carried him far to my left in a much more circumscribed circle than the hyaenodons had mapped out for him. Then I saw the female leap forward and head him; and when he would have gone too far to the left, Raja sprang, snapping, at his shoulder and held him straight.

Straight for me the two savage beasts were driving their quarry! It was wonderful.

It was something else, too, as I realized while the monstrous beast neared me. It was like standing in the middle of the tracks in front of an approaching express-train. But I didn't dare waver; too much depended upon my meeting that hurtling mass of terrified flesh with a well-placed javelin. So I stood there, waiting to be run down and crushed by those gigantic feet, but determined to drive home my weapon in the broad breast before I fell.

The lidi was only about a hundred yards from me when Raja gave a few barks in a tone that differed materially from his hunting-cry. Instantly both he and his mate leaped for the long neck of the ruminant.

Neither missed. Swinging in mid-air, they hung tenaciously, their weight dragging down the creature's head and so retarding its speed that before it had reached me it was almost stopped and devoting all its energies to attempting to scrape off its attackers with its forefeet.

Dian had seen and recognized me, and was trying to extricate herself from the grasp of her captor, who, handicapped by his strong and agile prisoner, was unable to wield his lance effectively upon the two jaloks. At the same time I was running swiftly toward them.

When the man discovered me he released his hold upon Dian and sprang to the ground, ready with his lance to meet me. My javelin was no match for his longer weapon, which was used more for stabbing than as a missile. Should I miss him at my first cast, as was quite probable, since he was prepared for me, I would have to face his formidable lance with nothing more than a stone knife. The outlook was scarcely entrancing. Evidently I was soon to be absolutely at his mercy.

Seeing my predicament, he ran toward me to get rid of one antagonist before he had to deal with the other two. He could not guess, of course, that the two jaloks were hunting with me; but he doubtless thought that after they had finished the lidi they would make after the human prey—the beasts are notorious killers, often slaying wantonly.

But as the Thurian came Raja loosened his hold upon the lidi and dashed for him, with the female close after. When the man saw them he yelled to me to help him, protesting that we should both be killed if we did not fight together. But I only laughed at him and ran toward Dian.

Both the fierce beasts were upon the Thurian simultaneously— he must have died almost before his body tumbled to the ground. Then the female wheeled toward Dian. I was standing by her side as the thing charged her, my javelin ready to receive her.

But again Raja was too quick for me. I imagine he thought she was making for me, for he couldn't have known anything of my relations toward Dian. At any rate he leaped full upon her back and dragged her down. There ensued forthwith as terrible a battle as one would wish to see if battles were gauged by volume of noise and riotousness of action. I thought that both the beasts would be torn to shreds.

When finally the female ceased to struggle and rolled over on her back, her forepaws limply folded, I was sure that she was dead. Raja stood over her, growling, his jaws close to her throat. Then I saw that neither of them bore a scratch. The male had simply administered a severe drubbing to his mate. It was his way of teaching her that I was sacred.

After a moment he moved away and let her rise, when she set about smoothing down her rumpled coat, while he came stalking toward Dian and me. I had an arm about Dian now. As Raja came close I caught him by the neck and pulled him up to me. There I stroked him and talked to him, bidding Dian do the same, until I think he pretty well understood that if I was his friend, so was Dian.

For a long time he was inclined to be shy of her, often baring his teeth at her approach, and it was a much longer time before the female made friends with us. But by careful kindness, by never eating without sharing our meat with them, and by feeding them from our hands, we finally won the confidence of both animals. However, that was a long time after.

With the two beasts trotting after us, we returned to where we had left Juag. Here I had the dickens' own time keeping the female from Juag's throat. Of all the venomous, wicked, cruel-hearted beasts on two worlds, I think a female hyaenodon takes the palm.

But eventually she tolerated Juag as she had Dian and me, and the five of us set out toward the coast, for Juag had just completed his labors on the thag when we arrived. We ate some of the meat before starting, and gave the hounds some. All that we could we carried upon our backs.

On the way to the canoe we met with no mishaps. Dian told me that the fellow who had stolen her had come upon her from behind while the roaring of the thag had drowned all other noises, and that the first she had known he had disarmed her and thrown her to the back of his lidi, which had been lying down close by waiting for him. By the time the thag had ceased bellowing the fellow had got well away upon his swift mount. By holding one palm over her mouth he had prevented her calling for help.

"I thought," she concluded, "that I should have to use the viper's tooth, after all."

We reached the beach at last and unearthed the canoe. Then we busied ourselves stepping a mast and rigging a small sail—Juag and I, that is—while Dian cut the thag meat into long strips for drying when we should be out in the sunlight once more.

At last all was done. We were ready to embark. I had no difficulty in getting Raja aboard the dugout; but Ranee—as we christened her after I had explained to Dian the meaning of Raja and its feminine equivalent—positively refused for a time to follow her mate aboard. In fact, we had to shove off without her. After a moment, however, she plunged into the water and swam after us.

I let her come alongside, and then Juag and I pulled her in, she snapping and snarling at us as we did so; but, strange to relate, she didn't offer to attack us after we had ensconced her safely in the bottom alongside Raja.

The canoe behaved much better under sail than I had hoped—infinitely better than the battle-ship *Sari* had—and we made good progress almost due west across the gulf, upon the opposite side of which I hoped to find the mouth of the river of which Juag had told me.

The islander was much interested and impressed by the sail and its results. He had not been able to understand exactly what I hoped to accomplish with it while we were fitting up the boat; but when he saw the clumsy dugout move steadily through the water without paddles, he was as delighted as a child. We made splendid headway on the trip, coming into sight of land at last.

Juag had been terror-stricken when he had learned that I intended crossing the ocean, and when we passed out of sight of land he was in a blue funk. He said that he had never heard of such a thing before in his life, and that always he had understood that those who ventured far from land never returned; for how could they find their way when they could see no land to steer for?

I tried to explain the compass to him; and though he never really grasped the scientific explanation of it, yet he did learn to steer by it quite as well as I. We passed several islands on the journey—islands which Juag told me were entirely unknown to his own island folk. Indeed, our eyes may have been the first ever to rest upon them. I should have liked to stop off and explore them, but the business of empire would brook no unnecessary delays.

I asked Juag how Hooja expected to reach the mouth of the river which we were in search of if he didn't cross the gulf, and the islander explained that Hooja would undoubtedly follow the coast around. For some time we sailed up the coast searching for the river, and at last we found it. So great was it that I thought it must be a mighty gulf until the mass of driftwood that came out upon the first ebb tide convinced me that it was the mouth of a river. There were the trunks of trees uprooted by the undermining of the river banks, giant creepers, flowers, grasses, and now and then the body of some land animal or bird.

I was all excitement to commence our upward journey when there occurred that which I had never before seen within Pellucidar—a really terrific wind-storm. It blew down the river upon us with a ferocity and suddenness that took our breaths away, and before we could get a chance to make the shore it became too late. The best that we could do was to hold the scudding craft before the wind and race along in a smother of white spume. Juag was terrified. If Dian was, she hid it; for was she not the daughter of a once great chief, the sister of a king, and the mate of an emperor?

Raja and Ranee were frightened. The former crawled close to my side and buried his nose against me. Finally even fierce Ranee was moved to seek sympathy from a human being. She slunk to Dian, pressing close against her and whimpering, while Dian stroked her shaggy neck and talked to her as I talked to Raja.

There was nothing for us to do but try to keep the canoe right side up and straight before the wind. For what seemed an eternity the tempest neither increased nor abated. I judged that we must have blown a hundred miles before the wind and straight out into an unknown sea!

As suddenly as the wind rose it died again, and when it died it veered to blow at right angles to its former course in a gentle breeze. I asked Juag then what our course was, for he had had the compass last. It had been on a leather thong about his neck. When he felt for it, the expression that came into his eyes told me as plainly as words what had happened—the compass was lost! The compass was lost!

And we were out of sight of land without a single celestial body to guide us! Even the pendent world was not visible from our position!

Our plight seemed hopeless to me, but I dared not let Dian and Juag guess how utterly dismayed I was; though, as I soon discovered, there was nothing to be gained by trying to keep the worst from Juag—he knew it quite as well as I. He had always known, from the legends of his people, the dangers of the open sea beyond the sight of land. The compass, since he had learned its uses from me, had been all that he had to buoy his hope of eventual salvation from the watery deep. He had seen how it had guided me across the water to the very coast that I desired to reach, and so he had implicit confidence in it. Now that it was gone, his confidence had departed, also.

There seemed but one thing to do; that was to keep on sailing straight before the wind—since we could travel most rapidly along that course—until we sighted land of some description. If it chanced to be the mainland, well and good; if an island—well, we might live upon an island. We certainly could not live long in this little boat, with only a few strips of dried thag and a few quarts of water left.

Quite suddenly a thought occurred to me. I was surprised that it had not come before as a solution to our problem. I turned toward Juag.

"You Pellucidarians are endowed with a wonderful instinct," I reminded him, "an instinct that points the way straight to your homes, no matter in what strange land you may find yourself. Now all we have to do is let Dian guide us toward Amoz, and we shall come in a short time to the same coast whence we just were blown."

As I spoke I looked at them with a smile of renewed hope; but there was no answering smile in their eyes. It was Dian who enlightened me.

"We could do all this upon land," she said. "But upon the water that power is denied us. I do not know why; but I have always heard that this is true—that only upon the water may a Pellucidarian be lost. This is, I think, why we all fear the great ocean so —even those who go upon its surface in canoes. Juag has told us that they never go beyond the sight of land."

We had lowered the sail after the blow while we were discussing the best course to pursue. Our little craft had been drifting idly, rising and falling with the great waves that were now diminishing. Sometimes we were upon the crest—again in the hollow. As Dian ceased speaking she let her eyes range across the limitless expanse of billowing waters. We rose to a great height upon the crest of a mighty wave. As we topped it Dian gave an exclamation and pointed astern.

"Boats!" she cried. "Boats! Many, many boats!"

Juag and I leaped to our feet; but our little craft had now dropped to the trough, and we could see nothing but walls of water close upon either hand. We waited for the next wave to lift us, and when it did we strained our eyes in the direction that Dian had indicated. Sure enough, scarce half a mile away were several boats, and scattered far and wide behind us as far as we could see were many others! We could not make them out in the distance or in the brief glimpse that we caught of them before we were plunged again into the next wave cañon; but they were boats.

And in them must be human beings like ourselves.

CHAPTER XIII

RACING FOR LIFE

AT LAST the sea subsided, and we were able to get a better view of the armada of small boats in our wake. There must have been two hundred of them. Juag said that he had never seen so many boats before in all his life. Where had they come from? Juag was first to hazard a guess.

"Hooja," he said, "was building many boats to carry his warriors to the great river and up it toward Sari. He was building them with almost all his warriors and many slaves upon the Island of Trees. No one else in all the history of Pellucidar has ever built so many boats as they told me Hooja was building. These must be Hooja's boats."

"And they were blown out to sea by the great storm just as we were," suggested Dian.

"There can be no better explanation of them," I agreed.

"What shall we do?" asked Juag.

"Suppose we make sure that they are really Hooja's people," suggested Dian. "It may be that they are not, and that if we run away from them before we learn definitely who they are, we shall be running away from a chance to live and find the mainland. They may be a people of whom we have never even heard, and if so we can ask them to help us—if they know the way to the mainland."

"Which they will not," interposed Juag.

"Well," I said, "it can't make our predicament any more trying to wait until we find out who they are. They are heading for us now. Evidently they have spied our sail, and guess that we do not belong to their fleet."

"They probably want to ask the way to the mainland themselves," said Juag, who was nothing if not a pessimist.

"If they want to catch us, they can do it if they can paddle faster than we can sail," I said. "If we let them come close enough to discover their identity, and can then sail faster than they can paddle, we can get away from them anyway, so we might as well wait."

And wait we did.

The sea calmed rapidly, so that by the time the foremost canoe had come within five hundred yards of us we could see them all plainly. Every one was headed for us. The dugouts, which were of unusual length, were manned by twenty paddlers, ten to a side. Besides the paddlers there were twenty-five or more warriors in each boat.

When the leader was a hundred yards from us Dian called our attention to the fact that several of her crew were Sagoths. That convinced us that the flotilla was indeed Hooja's. I told Juag to hail them and get what information he could, while I remained in the bottom of our canoe as much out of sight as possible. Dian lay down at full length in the bottom; I did not want them to see and recognize her if they were in truth Hooja's people.

"Who are you?" shouted Juag, standing up in the boat and making a megaphone of his palms.

A figure arose in the bow of the leading canoe—a figure that I was sure I recognized even before he spoke.

"I am Hooja!" cried the man, in answer to Juag.

For some reason he did not recognize his former prisoner and slave—possibly because he had so many of them.

"I come from the Island of Trees," he continued. "A hundred of my boats were lost in the great storm and all their crews drowned. Where is the land? What are you, and what strange thing is that which flutters from the little tree in the front of your canoe?"

He referred to our sail, flapping idly in the wind.

"We, too, are lost," replied Juag. "We know not where the land is. We are going back to look for it now."

So saying he commenced to scull the canoe's nose before the wind, while I made fast the primitive sheets that held our crude sail. We thought it time to be going.

There wasn't much wind at the time, and the heavy, lumbering dugout was slow in getting under way. I thought it never would gain any momentum. And all the while Hooja's canoe was drawing rapidly nearer, propelled by the strong arms of his twenty paddlers. Of course, their dugout was much larger than ours, and, consequently, infinitely heavier and more cumbersome; nevertheless, it was coming along at quite a clip, and ours was yet but barely moving. Dian and I remained out of sight as much as possible, for the two craft were now well within bow-shot of one another, and I knew that Hooja had archers.

Hooja called to Juag to stop when he saw that our craft was moving. He was much interested in the sail, and not a little awed, as I could tell by his shouted remarks and questions. Raising my head, I saw him plainly. He would have made an excellent target for one of my guns, and I had never been sorrier that I had lost them.

We were now picking up speed a trifle, and he was not gaining upon us so fast as at first. In consequence, his requests that we stop suddenly changed to commands as he became aware that we were trying to escape him.

"Come back!" he shouted. "Come back, or I'll fire!"

I use the word fire because it more nearly translates into English the Pellucidarian word *trag*, which covers the launching of any deadly missile.

But Juag only seized his paddle more tightly—the paddle that answered the purpose of rudder, and commenced to assist the wind by vigorous strokes. Then Hooja gave the command to some of his archers to fire upon us. I couldn't lie hidden in the bottom of the boat, leaving Juag alone exposed to the deadly shafts, so I arose and, seizing another paddle, set to work to help him. Dian joined me, though I did my best to persuade her to remain sheltered; but being a woman, she must have her own way.

The instant that Hooja saw us he recognized us. The whoop of triumph he raised indicated how certain he was that we were about to fall into his hands. A shower of arrows fell about us. Then Hooja caused his men to cease firing—he wanted us alive. None of the missiles struck us, for Hooja's archers were not nearly the marksmen that are my Sarians and Amozites.

We had now gained sufficient headway to hold our own on about even terms with Hooja's paddlers. We did not seem to be gaining, though; and neither did they. How long this nerve-racking experience lasted I cannot guess, though we had pretty nearly finished our meager supply of provisions when the wind picked up a bit and we commenced to draw away.

Not once yet had we sighted land, nor could I understand it, since so many of the seas I had seen before were thickly dotted with islands. Our plight was anything but pleasant, yet I think

that Hooja and his forces were even worse off than we, for they
had no food nor water at all.

Far out behind us in a long line that curved upward in the distance, to be lost in the haze, strung Hooja's two hundred boats.
But one would have been enough to have taken us could it have
come alongside. We had drawn some fifty yards ahead of Hooja—
there had been times when we were scarce ten yards in advance—
and were feeling considerably safer from capture. Hooja's men,
working in relays, were commencing to show the effects of the
strain under which they had been forced to work without food
or water, and I think their weakening aided us almost as much
as the slight freshening of the wind.

Hooja must have commenced to realize that he was going to lose
us, for he again gave orders that we be fired upon. Volley after
volley of arrows struck about us. The distance was so great by this
time that most of the arrows fell short, while those that reached us
were sufficiently spent to allow us to ward them off with our paddles. However, it was a most exciting ordeal.

Hooja stood in the bow of his boat, alternately urging his men
to greater speed and shouting epithets at me. But we continued
to draw away from him. At last the wind rose to a fair gale, and
we simply raced away from our pursuers as if they were standing
still. Juag was so tickled that he forgot all about his hunger and
thirst. I think that he had never been entirely reconciled to the
heathenish invention which I called a sail, and that down in the
bottom of his heart he believed that the paddlers would eventually overhaul us; but now he couldn't praise it enough.

We had a strong gale for a considerable time, and eventually
dropped Hooja's fleet so far astern that we could no longer discern
them. And then—ah, I shall never forget that moment—Dian
sprang to her feet with a cry of "Land!"

Sure enough, dead ahead, a long, low coast stretched across our
bow. It was still a long way off, and we couldn't make out whether
it was island or mainland; but at least it was land. If ever ship-
wrecked mariners were grateful, we were then. Raja and Ranee
were commencing to suffer for lack of food, and I could swear
that the latter often cast hungry glances upon us, though I am
equally sure that no such hideous thoughts ever entered the head
of her mate. We watched them both most closely, however. Once
while stroking Ranee I managed to get a rope around her neck
and make her fast to the side of the boat. Then I felt a bit safer
for Dian. It was pretty close quarters in that little dugout for three
human beings and two practically wild, man-eating dogs; but we

had to make the best of it, since I would not listen to Juag's suggestion that we kill and eat Raja and Ranee.

We made good time to within a few miles of the shore. Then the wind died suddenly out. We were all of us keyed up to such a pitch of anticipation that the blow was doubly hard to bear. And it was a blow, too, since we could not tell in what quarter the wind might rise again; but Juag and I set to work to paddle the remaining distance.

Almost immediately the wind rose again from precisely the opposite direction from which it had formerly blown, so that it was mighty hard work making progress against it. Next it veered again so that we had to turn and run with it parallel to the coast to keep from being swamped in the trough of the seas.

And while we were suffering all these disappointments Hooja's fleet appeared in the distance!

They evidently had gone far to the left of our course, for they were now almost behind us as we ran parallel to the coast; but we were not much afraid of being overtaken in the wind that was blowing. The gale kept on increasing, but it was fitful, swooping down upon us in great gusts and then going almost calm for an instant. It was after one of these momentary calms that the catastrophe occurred. Our sail hung limp and our momentum decreased when of a sudden a particularly vicious squall caught us. Before I could cut the sheets the mast had snapped at the thwart in which it was stepped.

The worst had happened; Juag and I seized paddles and kept the canoe with the wind; but that squall was the parting shot of the gale, which died out immediately after, leaving us free to make for the shore, which we lost no time in attempting. But Hooja had drawn closer in toward shore than we, so it looked as if he might head us off before we could land. However, we did our best to distance him, Dian taking a paddle with us.

We were in a fair way to succeed when there appeared, pouring from among the trees beyond the beach, a horde of yelling, painted savages, brandishing all sorts of devilish-looking primitive weapons. So menacing was their attitude that we realized at once the folly of attempting to land among them.

Hooja was drawing closer to us. We could not hope to outpaddle him. And with our sail gone, no wind would help us, though, as if in derision at our plight, a steady breeze was now blowing. But we had no intention of sitting idle while our fate overtook us, so we bent to our paddles and, keeping parallel with the coast, did our best to pull away from our pursuers.

It was a grueling experience. We were weakened by lack of food. We were suffering the pangs of thirst. Capture and death were close at hand. Yet I think that we gave a good account of ourselves in our final effort to escape. Our boat was so much smaller and lighter than any of Hooja's that the three of us forced it ahead almost as rapidly as his larger craft could go under their twenty paddles.

As we raced along the coast for one of those seemingly interminable periods that may draw hours into eternities where the labor is soul-searing and there is no way to measure time, I saw what I took for the opening to a bay or the mouth of a great river a short distance ahead of us. I wished that we might make for it; but with the menace of Hooja close behind and the screaming natives who raced along the shore parallel to us, I dared not attempt it.

We were not far from shore in that mad flight from death. Even as I paddled I found opportunity to glance occasionally toward the natives. They were white, but hideously painted. From their gestures and weapons I took them to be a most ferocious race. I was rather glad that we had not succeeded in landing among them.

Hooja's fleet had been in much more compact formation when we sighted them this time than on the occasion following the tempest. Now they were moving rapidly in pursuit of us, all well within the radius of a mile. Five of them were leading, all abreast, and were scarce two hundred yards from us. When I glanced over my shoulder I could see that the archers had already fitted arrows to their bows in readiness to fire upon us the moment that they should draw within range.

Hope was low in my breast. I could not see the slightest chance of escaping them, for they were overhauling us rapidly now, since they were able to work their paddles in relays, while we three were rapidly wearying beneath the constant strain that had been put upon us.

It was then that Juag called my attention to the rift in the shoreline which I had thought either a bay or the mouth of a great river. There I saw moving slowly out into the sea that which filled my soul with wonder.

CHAPTER XIV

GORE AND DREAMS

IT WAS a two-masted felucca with lateen sails! The craft was long and low. In it were more than fifty men, twenty or thirty of whom were at oars with which the craft was being propelled from the lee of the land. I was dumbfounded.

Could it be that the savage, painted natives I had seen on shore had so perfected the art of navigation that they were masters of such advanced building and rigging as this craft proclaimed? It seemed impossible! And as I looked I saw another of the same type swing into view and follow its sister through the narrow strait out into the ocean.

Nor were these all. One after another, following closely upon one another's heels, came fifty of the trim, graceful vessels. They were cutting in between Hooja's fleet and our little dugout.

When they came a bit closer my eyes fairly popped from my head at what I saw, for in the eye of the leading felucca stood a man with a sea-glass leveled upon us. Who could they be? Was there a civilization within Pellucidar of such wondrous advancement as this? Were there far-distant lands of which none of my people had ever heard, where a race had so greatly outstripped all other races of this inner world?

The man with the glass had lowered it and was shouting to us. I could not make out his words, but presently I saw that he was pointing aloft. When I looked I saw a pennant fluttering from the peak of the forward lateen yard—a red, white, and blue pennant, with a single great white star in a field of blue.

Then I knew. My eyes went even wider than they had before. It was the navy! It was the navy of the empire of Pellucidar which I had instructed Perry to build in my absence. It was *my* navy!

I dropped my paddle and stood up and shouted and waved my hand. Juag and Dian looked at me as if I had gone suddenly mad. When I could stop shouting I told them, and they shared my joy and shouted with me.

But still Hooja was coming nearer, nor could the leading felucca overhaul him before he would be alongside or at least within bow-shot.

Hooja must have been as much mystified as we were as to the identity of the strange fleet; but when he saw me waving to them he evidently guessed that they were friendly to us, so he urged his men to redouble their efforts to reach us before the felucca cut him off.

He shouted word back to others of his fleet—word that was passed back until it had reached them all—directing them to run alongside the strangers and board them, for with his two hundred craft and his eight or ten thousand warriors he evidently felt equal to overcoming the fifty vessels of the enemy, which did not seem to carry over three thousand men all told.

His own personal energies he bent to reaching Dian and me first, leaving the rest of the work to his other boats. I thought that there could be little doubt that he would be successful in so far as we were concerned, and I feared for the revenge that he might take upon us should the battle go against his force, as I was sure it would; for I knew that Perry and his Mezops must have brought with them all the arms and ammunition that had been contained in the prospector. But I was not prepared for what happened next.

As Hooja's canoe reached a point some twenty yards from us a great puff of smoke broke from the bow of the leading felucca, followed almost simultaneously by a terrific explosion, and a solid shot screamed close over the heads of the men in Hooja's craft, raising a great splash where it clove the water just beyond them.

Perry had perfected gunpowder and built cannon! It was marvelous! Dian and Juag, as much surprised as Hooja, turned wondering eyes toward me. Again the cannon spoke. I suppose that by comparison with the great guns of modern naval vessels of the outer world it was a pitifully small and inadequate thing; but here in Pellucidar, where it was the first of its kind, it was about as awe-inspiring as anything you might imagine.

With the report an iron cannon-ball about five inches in diameter struck Hooja's dugout just above the water-line, tore a great splintering hole in its side, turned it over, and dumped its occupants into the sea.

The four dugouts that had been abreast of Hooja had turned to intercept the leading felucca. Even now, in the face of what must have been a withering catastrophe to them, they kept bravely on toward the strange and terrible craft.

In them were fully two hundred men, while but fifty lined the gunwale of the felucca to repel them. The commander of the felucca, who proved to be Ja, let them come quite close and then turned loose upon them a volley of shots from small-arms.

The cave men and Sagoths in the dugouts seemed to wither before that blast of death like dry grass before a prairie fire. Those who were not hit dropped their bows and javelins and, seizing upon paddles, attempted to escape. But the felucca pursued them relentlessly, her crew firing at will.

At last I heard Ja shouting to the survivors in the dugouts—they were all quite close to us now—offering them their lives if they would surrender. Perry was standing close behind Ja, and I knew that this merciful action was prompted, perhaps commanded, by the old man; for no Pellucidarian would have thought of showing leniency to a defeated foe.

As there was no alternative save death, the survivors surrendered and a moment later were taken aboard the *Amoz*, the name that I could now see printed in large letters upon the felucca's bow, and which no one in that whole world could read except Perry and I.

When the prisoners were aboard, Ja brought the felucca alongside our dugout. Many were the willing hands that reached down to lift us to her decks. The bronze faces of the Mezops were broad with smiles, and Perry was fairly beside himself with joy.

Dian went aboard first and then Juag, as I wished to help Raja and Ranee aboard myself, well knowing that it would fare ill with any Mezop who touched them. We got them aboard at last, and a great commotion they caused among the crew, who had never seen a wild beast thus handled by man before.

Perry and Dian and I were so full of questions that we fairly burst, but we had to contain ourselves for a while, since the battle with the rest of Hooja's fleet had scarce commenced. From the small forward decks of the feluccas Perry's crude cannon were belching smoke, flame, thunder, and death. The air trembled to the roar of them. Hooja's horde, intrepid, savage fighters that they were, were closing in to grapple in a last death-struggle with the Mezops who manned our vessels.

The handling of our fleet by the red island warriors of Ja's clan was far from perfect. I could see that Perry had lost no time after the completion of the boats in setting out upon this cruise. What little the captains and crews had learned of handling feluccas they must have learned principally since they embarked upon this voyage, and while experience is an excellent teacher and had done much for them, they still had a great deal to learn. In maneuvering for position they were continually fouling one another, and on two occasions shots from our batteries came near to striking our own ships.

No sooner, however, was I aboard the flagship than I attempted to rectify this trouble to some extent. By passing commands by word of mouth from one ship to another I managed to get the fifty feluccas into some sort of line, with the flag-ship in the lead. In this formation we commenced slowly to circle the position of the enemy. The dugouts came for us right along in an attempt to board us, but by keeping on the move in one direction and circling, we managed to avoid getting in each other's way, and were enabled to fire our cannon and our small arms with less danger to our own comrades.

When I had a moment to look about me, I took in the felucca on which I was. I am free to confess that I marveled at the excellent construction and stanch yet speedy lines of the little craft. That Perry had chosen this type of vessel seemed rather remarkable, for though I had warned him against turreted battle-ships, armor, and like useless show, I had fully expected that when I beheld his navy I should find considerable attempt at grim and terrible magnificence, for it was always Perry's idea to overawe these ignorant cave men when we had to contend with them in battle. But I had soon learned that while one might easily astonish them with some new engine of war, it was an utter impossibility to frighten them into surrender.

I learned later that Ja had gone carefully over the plans of various craft with Perry. The old man had explained in detail all that the text told him of them. The two had measured out dimensions upon the ground, that Ja might see the sizes of different boats. Perry had built models, and Ja had had him read carefully and explain all that they could find relative to the handling of sailing vessels. The result of this was that Ja was the one who had chosen the felucca. It was well that Perry had had so excellent a balance-wheel, for he had been wild to build a huge frigate of the Nelsonian era—he told me so himself.

One thing that had inclined Ja particularly to the felucca was the fact that it included oars in its equipment. He realized the limitations of his people in the matter of sails, and while they had never used oars, the implement was so similar to a paddle that he was sure they quickly could master the art—and they did. As soon as one hull was completed Ja kept it on the water constantly, first with one crew and then with another, until two thousand red warriors had learned to row. Then they stepped their masts and a crew was told off for the first ship.

While the others were building they learned to handle theirs. As each succeeding boat was launched its crew took it out and practiced with it under the tutorage of those who had graduated from the first ship, and so on until a full complement of men had been trained for every boat.

Well, to get back to the battle: The Hoojans kept on coming at us, and as fast as they came we mowed them down. It was little else than slaughter. Time and time again I cried to them to surrender, promising them their lives if they would do so. At last there were but ten boatloads left. These turned in flight. They thought they could paddle away from us—it was pitiful! I passed the word from boat to boat to cease firing—not to kill another Hoojan unless they fired on us. Then we set out after them. There was a nice little breeze blowing and we bowled along after our quarry as gracefully and as lightly as swans upon a park lagoon. As we approached them I could see not only wonder but admiration in their eyes. I hailed the nearest dugout.

"Throw down your arms and come aboard us," I cried, "and you shall not be harmed. We will feed you and return you to the mainland. Then you shall go free upon your promise never to bear arms against the Emperor of Pellucidar again!"

I think it was the promise of food that interested them most. They could scarce believe that we would not kill them. But when I exhibited the prisoners we already had taken, and showed them that they were alive and unharmed, a great Sagoth in one of the boats asked me what guarantee I could give that I would keep my word.

"None other than my word," I replied. "That I do not break."

The Pellucidarians themselves are rather punctilious about this same matter, so the Sagoth could understand that I might possibly be speaking the truth. But he could not understand why we should not kill them unless we meant to enslave them, which I had as much as denied already when I had promisd to set them free. Ja couldn't exactly see the wisdom of my plan, either. He thought that we ought to follow up the ten remaining dugouts and sink them all; but I insisted that we must free as many as possible of our enemies upon the mainland.

"You see," I explained, "these men will return at once to Hooja's Island, to the Mahar cities from which they come, or to the countries from which they were stolen by the Mahars. They are men of two races and of many countries. They will spread the story of our victory far and wide, and while they are with us, we will let them see and hear many other wonderful things which they may carry back to their friends and their chiefs. It's the finest chance for free publicity, Perry," I added to the old man, "that you or I have seen in many a day."

Perry agreed with me. As a matter of fact, he would have agreed to anything that would have restrained us from killing the poor devils who fell into our hands. He was a great fellow to invent gunpowder and firearms and cannon; but when it came to using these things to kill people, he was as tenderhearted as a chicken.

The Sagoth who had spoken was talking to other Sagoths in his boat. Evidently they were holding a council over the question of the wisdom of surrendering.

"What will become of you if you don't surrender to us?" I asked. "If we do not open up our batteries on you again and kill you all, you will simply drift about the sea helplessly until you die of thirst and starvation. You cannot return to the islands, for you have seen as well as we that the natives there are very numerous and warlike. They would kill you the moment you landed."

The upshot of it was that the boat of which the Sagoth speaker was in charge surrendered. The Sagoths threw down their weapons, and we took them aboard the ship next in line behind the *Amoz*. First Ja had to impress upon the captain and crew of the ship that the prisoners were not to be abused or killed. After that the remaining dugouts paddled up and surrendered. We distributed them among the entire fleet lest there be too many upon any one vessel. Thus ended the first real naval engagement that the Pellucidarian seas had ever witnessed—though Perry still insists that the action in which the *Sari* took part was a battle of the first magnitude.

The battle over and the prisoners disposed of and fed—and do not imagine that Dian, Juag, and I, as well as the two hounds were not fed also—I turned my attention to the fleet. We had the feluccas close in about the flag-ship, and with all the ceremony of a medieval potentate on parade I received the commanders of the forty-nine feluccas that accompanied the flag-ship—Dian and I together—the empress and the emperor of Pellucidar.

It was a great occasion. The savage, bronze warriors entered into the spirit of it, for as I learned later dear old Perry had left no opportunity neglected for impressing upon them that David was emperor of Pellucidar, and that all that they were accomplishing and all that he was accomplishing was due to the power, and redounded to the glory of David. The old man must have rubbed it in pretty strong, for those fierce warriors nearly came to blows in their efforts to be among the first of those to kneel before me and kiss my hand. When it came to kissing Dian's I think they enjoyed it more; I know I should have.

A happy thought occurred to me as I stood upon the little deck of the *Amoz* with the first of Perry's primitive cannon behind me. When Ja kneeled at my feet, the first to do me homage, I drew from its scabbard at his side the sword of hammered iron that Perry had taught him to fashion. Striking him lightly on the shoulder I created him king of Anoroc. Each captain of the forty-nine other feluccas I made a duke. I left it to Perry to enlighten them as to the value of the honors I had bestowed upon them.

During these ceremonies Raja and Ranee had stood beside Dian and me. Their bellies had been well filled, but still they had difficulty in permitting so much edible humanity to pass unchallenged. It was a good education for them though, and never after did they find it difficult to associate with the human race without arousing their appetites.

After the ceremonies were over we had a chance to talk with Perry and Ja. The former told me that Ghak, king of Sari, had sent my letter and map to him by a runner, and that he and Ja had at once decided to set out, on the completion of the fleet, to ascertain the correctness of my theory that the Lural Az, in which the Anoroc Islands lay, was in reality the same ocean as that which lapped the shores of Thuria under the name of Sojar Az, or Great Sea.

Their destination had been the island retreat of Hooja, and they had sent word to Ghak of their plans that we might work in harmony with them. The tempest that had blown us off the coast of the continent had blown them far to the south also. Shortly before discovering us they had come into a great group of islands, from between the largest two of which they were sailing when they saw Hooja's fleet pursuing our dugout.

I asked Perry if he had any idea as to where we were, or in what direction lay Hooja's island or the continent. He replied by producing his map, on which he had carefully marked the newly discovered islands—there described as the Unfriendly Isles—which showed Hooja's island northwest of us about two points west.

He then explained that with compass, chronometer, log and reel, they had kept a fairly accurate record of their course from the time they had set out. Four of the feluccas were equipped with these instruments, and all of the captains had been instructed in their use.

I was very greatly surprised at the ease with which these savages had mastered the rather intricate detail of this unusual work, but Perry assured me that they were a wonderfully intelligent race, and had been quick to grasp all that he had tried to teach them.

Another thing that surprised me was the fact that so much had been accomplished in so short a time, for I could not believe that I had been gone from Anoroc for a sufficient period to permit of building a fleet of fifty feluccas and mining iron ore for the cannon and balls, to say nothing of manufacturing these guns and the crude muzzle-loading rifles with which every Mezop was armed, as well as the gunpowder and ammunition they had in such ample quantities.

"Time!" exclaimed Perry. "Well, how long *were* you gone from Anoroc before we picked you up in the Sojar Az?"

That was a puzzler, and I had to admit it. I didn't know how much time had elapsed and neither did Perry, for time is nonexistent in Pellucidar.

"Then, you see, David," he continued, "I had almost unbelievable resources at my disposal. The Mezops inhabiting the Anoroc Islands, which stretch far out to sea beyond the three principal isles with which you are familiar, number well into the millions, and by far the greater part of them are friendly to Ja. Men, women, and children turned to and worked the moment Ja explained the nature of our enterprise.

"And not only were they anxious to do all in their power to hasten the day when the Mahars should be overthrown, but— and this counted for most of all—they are simply ravenous for greater knowledge and for better ways of doing things.

"The contents of the prospector set their imaginations to working overtime, so that they craved to own, themselves, the knowledge which had made it possible for other men to create and build the things which you brought back from the outer world.

"And then," continued the old man, "the element of time, or, rather, lack of time, operated to my advantage. There being no nights, there was no laying off from work—they labored incessantly, stopping only to eat and, on rare occasions, to sleep. Once we had discovered iron ore we had enough mined in an incredibly short time to build a thousand cannon. I had only to show them once how a thing should be done, and they would fall to work by thousands to do it.

"Why, no sooner had we fashioned the first muzzle-loader and they had seen it work successfully, than fully three thousand Mezops fell to work to make rifles. Of course there was much confusion and lost motion at first, but eventually Ja got them in hand, detailing squads of them under competent chiefs to certain work.

"We now have a hundred expert gunmakers. On a little isolated isle we have a great powder-factory. Near the iron-mine, which is on the mainland, is a smelter, and on the eastern shore of Anoroc, a well equipped shipyard. All these industries are

guarded by forts in which several cannon are mounted and where
warriors are always on guard.

"You would be surprised now, David, at the aspect of Anoroc.
I am surprised myself; it seems always to me as I compare it with
the day that I first set foot upon it from the deck of the *Sari* that
only a miracle could have worked the change that has taken place."

"It is a miracle," I said; "it is nothing short of a miracle to trans-
plant all the wondrous possibilities of the twentieth century back
to the Stone Age. It is a miracle to think that only five hundred
miles of earth separate two epochs that are really ages and ages
apart.

"It is stupendous, Perry! But still more stupendous is the power
that you and I wield in this great world. These people look upon
us as little less than supermen. We must show them that we are
all of that.

"We must give them the best that we have, Perry."

"Yes," he agreed; "we must. I have been thinking a great deal
lately that some kind of shrapnel shell or explosive bomb would
be a most splendid innovation in their warfare. Then there are
breech-loading rifles and those with magazines that I must hasten
to study out and learn to reproduce as soon as we get settled down
again; and——"

"Hold on, Perry!" I cried. "I didn't mean these sorts of things
at all. I said that we must give them the best we have. What we
have given them so far has been the worst. We have given them
war and the munitions of war. In a single day we have made their
wars infinitely more terrible and bloody than in all their past ages
they have been able to make them with their crude, primitive
weapons.

"In a period that could scarcely have exceeded two outer earthly
hours, our fleet practically annihilated the largest armada of native
canoe that the Pellucidarians ever before had gathered together.
We butchered some eight thousand warriors with the twentieth-
century gifts we brought. Why, they wouldn't have killed that
many warriors in the entire duration of a dozen of their wars with
their own weapons! No, Perry; we've got to give them something
better than scientific methods of killing one another."

The old man looked at me in amazement. There was reproach
in his eyes, too.

"Why, David!" he said sorrowfully. "I thought that you would
be pleased with what I had done. We planned these things together, and I am sure that it was you who suggested practically all

of it. I have done only what I thought you wished done and I have done it the best that I know how."

I laid my hand on the old man's shoulder.

"Bless your heart, Perry!" I cried. "You've accomplished miracles. You have done precisely what I should have done, only you've done it better. I'm not finding fault; but I don't wish to lose sight myself, or let you lose sight, of the greater work which must grow out of this preliminary and necessary carnage. First we must place the empire upon a secure footing, and we can do so only by putting the fear of us in the hearts of our enemies; but after that——

"Ah, Perry! That is the day I look forward to! When you and I can build sewing-machines instead of battle-ships, harvesters of crops instead of harvesters of men, plowshares and telephones, schools and colleges, printing-presses and paper! When our merchant marine shall ply the great Pellucidarian seas, and cargoes of silks and typewriters and books shall forge their ways where only hideous saurians have held sway since time began!"

"Amen!" said Perry.

And Dian, who was standing at my side, pressed my hand.

CHAPTER XV

CONQUEST AND PEACE

THE fleet sailed directly for Hooja's island, coming to anchor at its northeastern extremity before the flat-topped hill that had been Hooja's stronghold. I sent one of the prisoners ashore to demand an immediate surrender; but as he told me afterward they wouldn't believe all that he told them, so they congregated on the cliff-top and shot futile arrows at us.

In reply I had five of the feluccas cannonade them. When they scampered away at the sound of the terrific explosions and at sight of the smoke and the iron balls, I landed a couple of hundred red warriors and led them to the opposite end of the hill into the tunnel that ran to its summit. Here we met a little resistance; but a volley from the muzzle-loaders turned back those who disputed our right of way, and presently we gained the mesa. Here again we met resistance, but at last the remnant of Hooja's horde surrendered.

Juag was with me, and I lost no time in returning to him and his tribe the hilltop that had been their ancestral home for ages until they were robbed of it by Hooja. I created a kingdom of the island, making Juag king there. Before we sailed I went to Gr-gr-gr, chief of the beast-men, taking Juag with me. There the three of us arranged a code of laws that would permit the brute-folk and the human beings of the island to live in peace and harmony. Gr-gr-gr sent his son with me back to Sari, capital of my empire, that he might learn the ways of the human beings. I have hopes of turning this race into the greatest agriculturists of Pellucidar.

When I returned to the fleet I found that one of the islanders of Juag's tribe, who had been absent when we arrived, had just returned from the mainland with the news that a great army was encamped in the Land of Awful Shadow, and that they were threatening Thuria. I lost no time in weighing anchors and setting out for the continent, which we reached after a short and easy voyage.

From the deck of the *Amoz* I scanned the shore through the glasses that Perry had brought with him. When we were close enough for the glasses to be of value I saw that there was indeed a vast concourse of warriors entirely encircling the walled village of Goork, chief of the Thurians. As we approached smaller objects became distinguishable. It was then that I discovered numerous flags and pennants floating above the army of the besiegers.

I called Perry and passed the glasses to him.

"Ghak of Sari," I said.

Perry looked through the lenses for a moment, and then turned to me with a smile.

"The red, white, and blue of the empire," he said. "It is indeed your majesty's army."

It soon became apparent that we had been sighted by those on shore, for a great multitude of warriors had congregated along the beach watching us. We came to anchor as close in as we dared, which with our light feluccas was within easy speaking-distance of the shore. Ghak was there and his eyes were mighty wide, too; for, as he told us later, though he knew this must be Perry's fleet it was so wonderful to him that he could not believe the testimony of his own eyes even while he was watching it approach.

To give the proper effect to our meeting I commanded that each felucca fire twenty-one guns as a salute to His Majesty Ghak, King of Sari. Some of the gunners, in the exuberance of their enthusiasm, fired solid shot; but fortunately they had sufficient good judgment to train their pieces on the open sea, so no harm was done. After this we landed—an arduous task since each felucca carried but a single light dugout.

I learned from Ghak that the Thurian chieftain, Goork, had been inclined to haughtiness, and had told Ghak, the Hairy One, that he knew nothing of me and cared less; but I imagine that the sight of the fleet and the sound of the guns brought him to his senses, for it was not long before he sent a deputation to me, inviting me to visit him in his village. Here he apologized for the treatment he had accorded me, very gladly swore allegiance to the empire, and received in return the title of king.

We remained in Thuria only long enough to arrange the treaty with Goork, among the other details of which was his promise to furnish the imperial army with a thousand lidi, or Thurian beasts of burden, and drivers for them. These were to accompany Ghak's army back to Sari by land, while the fleet sailed to the mouth of the great river from which Dian, Juag, and I had been blown.

The voyage was uneventful. We found the river easily, and sailed up it for many miles through as rich and wonderful a plain as I have ever seen. At the head of navigation we disembarked, leaving a sufficient guard for the feluccas, and marched the remaining distance to Sari.

Ghak's army, which was composed of warriors of all the original tribes of the federation, showing how successful had been his efforts to rehabilitate the empire, marched into Sari some time after we arrived. With them were the thousand lidi from Thuria.

At a council of the kings it was decided that we should at once commence the great war against the Mahars, for these haughty reptiles presented the greatest obstacle to human progress within Pellucidar. I laid out a plan of campaign which met with the enthusiastic indorsement of the kings. Pursuant to it, I at once despatched fifty lidi to the fleet with orders to fetch fifty cannon to Sari. I also ordered the fleet to proceed at once to Anoroc, where they were to take aboard all the rifles and ammunition that had been completed since their departure, and with a full complement of men to sail along the coast in an attempt to find a passage to the inland sea near which lay the Mahars' buried city of Phutra.

Ja was sure that a large and navigable river connected the sea of Phutra with the Lural Az, and that, barring accident, the fleet would be before Phutra as soon as the land forces were.

At last the great army started upon its march. There were warriors from every one of the federated kingdoms. All were armed either with bow and arrows or muzzle-loaders, for nearly the entire Mezop contingent had been enlisted for this march, only sufficient having been left aboard the feluccas to man them properly. I divided the forces into divisions, regiments, battalions, companies, and even to platoons and sections, appointing the full complement of officers and non-commissioned officers. On the long march I schooled them in their duties, and as fast as one learned I sent him among the others as a teacher.

Each regiment was made up of about a thousand bowmen, and to each was temporarily attached a company of Mezop musketeers and a battery of artillery—the latter, our naval guns, mounted upon the broad backs of the mighty lidi. There was also one full regiment of Mezop musketeers and a regiment of primitive spearmen. The rest of the lidi that we brought with us were used for baggage animals and to transport our women and children, for we had brought them with us, as it was our intention to march from one Mahar city to another until we had subdued every Mahar nation that menaced the safety of any kingdom of the empire.

Before we reached the plain of Phutra we were discovered by a company of Sagoths, who at first stood to give battle; but upon seeing the vast numbers of our army they turned and fled toward Phutra. The result of this was that when we came in sight of the hundred towers which mark the entrances to the buried city we found a great army of Sagoths and Mahars lined up to give us battle.

At a thousand yards we halted, and, placing our artillery upon a slight eminence at either flank, we commenced to drop solid shot among them. Ja, who was chief artillery officer, was in command of this branch of the service, and he did some excellent work, for his Mezop gunners had become rather proficient by this time. The Sagoths couldn't stand much of this sort of warfare, so they charged us, yelling like fiends. We let them come quite close, and then the musketeers who formed the first line opened up on them.

The slaughter was something frightful, but still the remnants of them kept on coming until it was a matter of hand-to-hand fighting. Here our spearmen were of value, as were also the crude iron swords with which most of the imperial warriors were armed.

We lost heavily in the encounter after the Sagoths reached us; but they were absolutely exterminated—not one remained even as a prisoner. The Mahars, seeing how the battle was going, had hastened to the safety of their buried city. When we had overcome their gorilla-men we followed after them.

But here we were doomed to defeat, at least temporarily; for no sooner had the first of our troops descended into the subterranean avenues than many of them came stumbling and fighting their way back to the surface, half-choked by the fumes of some deadly gas that the reptiles had liberated upon them. We lost a number of men here. Then I sent for Perry, who had remained discreetly in the rear, and had him construct a little affair that I had had in my mind against the possibility of our meeting with a check at the entrances to the underground city.

Under my direction he stuffed one of his cannon full of powder, small bullets, and pieces of stone, almost to the muzzle. Then he plugged the muzzle tight with a cone-shaped block of wood, hammered and jammed in as tight as it could be. Next he inserted a long fuse. A dozen men rolled the cannon to the top of the stairs leading down into the city, first removing it from its carriage. One of them lit the fuse and the whole thing was given a smart shove down the stairway, while the detachment turned and scampered to a safe distance.

For what seemed a very long time nothing happened. We had commenced to think that the fuse had been put out while the piece was rolling down the stairway, or that the Mahars had guessed its purpose and extinguished it themselves, when the ground about the entrance rose suddenly into the air, to be followed by a terrific explosion and a burst of smoke and flame that shot high in company with dirt, stone, and fragments of cannon.

Perry had been working on two more of these giant bombs as soon as the first was completed. Presently we launched these into two of the other entrances. They were all that were required, for almost immediately after the third explosion a stream of Mahars broke from the exits furthest from us, rose upon their wings, and soared northward. A hundred men on lidi were despatched in pursuit, each lidi carrying two riflemen in addition to its driver. Guessing that the inland sea, which lay not far north of Phutra, was their destination, I took a couple of regiments and followed.

A low ridge intervenes between the Phutra plain where the city lies, and the inland sea where the Mahars were wont to disport themselves in the cool waters. Not until we had topped this ridge did we get a view of the sea.

Then we beheld a scene that I shall never forget so long as I may live.

Along the beach were lined up the troop of lidi, while a hundred yards from shore the surface of the water was black with the long snouts and cold, reptilian eyes of the Mahars. Our savage Mezop riflemen, and the shorter, squatter, white-skinned Thurian drivers, shading their eyes with their hands, were gazing seaward beyond the Mahars, whose eyes were fastened upon the same spot.

My heart leaped when I discovered that which was chaining the attention of them all. Twenty graceful feluccas were moving smoothly across the waters of the sea toward the reptilian horde!

The sight must have filled the Mahars with awe and consternation, for never had they seen the like of these craft before. For a time they seemed unable to do aught but gaze at the approaching fleet; but when the Mezops opened on them with their muskets the reptiles swam rapidly in the direction of the feluccas, evidently thinking that these would prove the easier to overcome. The commander of the fleet permitted them to approach within a hundred yards. Then he opened on them with all the cannon that could be brought to bear, as well as with the small arms of the sailors.

A great many of the reptiles were killed at the first volley. They wavered for a moment, then dived; nor did we see them again for a long time.

But finally they rose far out beyond the fleet, and when the feluccas came about and pursued them they left the water and flew away toward the north.

Following the fall of Phutra I visited Anoroc, where I found the people busy in the shipyards and the factories that Perry had established. I discovered something, too, that he had not told me of —something that seemed infinitely more promising than the powder-factory or the arsenal. It was a young man poring over one of the books I had brought back from the outer world! He was sitting in the log cabin that Perry had had built to serve as his sleeping quarters and office. So absorbed was he that he did not notice our entrance. Perry saw the look of astonishment in my eyes and smiled.

"I started teaching him the alphabet when we first reached the prospector, and were taking out its contents," he explained. "He was much mystified by the books and anxious to know of what use they were. When I explained he asked me to teach him to read, and so I worked with him whenever I could. He is very intelligent and learns quickly. Before I left he had made great progress, and as soon as he is qualified he is going to teach others to read. It was mighty hard work getting started, though, for everything had to be translated into Pellucidarian.

"It will take a long time to solve this problem, but I think that by teaching a number of them to read and write English we shall then be able more quickly to give them a written language of their own."

And this was the nucleus about which we were to build our great system of schools and colleges—this almost naked red warrior, sitting in Perry's little cabin upon the island of Anoroc, picking out words letter by letter from a work on intensive farming. Now we have——

But I'll get to all that before I finish.

While we were at Anoroc I accompanied Ja in an expedition to South Island, the southernmost of the three largest which form the Anoroc group—Perry had given it its name—where we made peace with the tribe there that had for long been hostile toward Ja. They were now glad enough to make friends with him and come into the federation. From there we sailed with sixty-five feluccas for distant Luana, the main island of the group where dwell the hereditary enemies of Anoroc.

Twenty-five of the feluccas were of a new and larger type than those with which Ja and Perry had sailed on the occasion when they chanced to find and rescue Dian and me. They were longer, carried much larger sails, and were considerably swifter. Each carried four guns instead of two, and these were so arranged that one or more of them could be brought into action no matter where the enemy lay.

The Luana group lies just beyond the range of vision from the mainland. The largest island of it alone is visible from Anoroc; but when we neared it we found that it comprised many beautiful islands, and that they were thickly populated. The Luanians had not, of course, been ignorant of all that had been going on in the domains of their nearest and dearest enemies. They knew of our feluccas and our guns, for several of their raiding-parties had had a taste of both. But their principal chief, an old man, had never seen either. So, when he sighted us, he put out to overwhelm us, bringing with him a fleet of about a hundred large war-canoes, loaded to capacity with javelin-armed warriors. It was pitiful, and I told Ja as much. It seemed a shame to massacre these poor fellows if there was any way out of it.

To my surprise Ja felt much as I did. He said he had always hated to war with other Mezops when there were so many alien races to fight against. I suggested that we hail the chief and request a parley; but when Ja did so the old fool thought that we were afraid, and with loud cries of exultation urged his warriors upon us.

So we opened up on them, but at my suggestion centered our fire upon the chief's canoe. The result was that in about thirty seconds there was nothing left of that war dugout but a handful of splinters, while its crew—those who were not killed—were struggling in the water, battling with the myriad terrible creatures that had risen to devour them.

We saved some of them, but the majority died just as had Hooja and the crew of his canoe that time our second shot capsized them.

Again we called to the remaining warriors to enter into a parley with us; but the chief's son was there and he would not, now that he had seen his father killed. He was all for revenge. So we had to open up on the brave fellows with all our guns; but it didn't last long at that, for there chanced to be wiser heads among the Luanians than their chief or his son had possessed. Presently an old warrior who commanded one of the dugouts surrendered. After that they came in one by one until all had laid their weapons upon our decks.

Then we called together upon the flag-ship all our captains, to give the affair greater weight and dignity, and all the principal men of Luana. We had conquered them, and they expected either death or slavery; but they deserved neither, and I told them so. It is always my habit here in Pellucidar to impress upon these savage people that mercy is as noble a quality as physical bravery, and that next to the men who fight shoulder to shoulder with us, we should honor the brave men who fight against us, and if we are victorious, award them both the mercy and honor that are their due.

By adhering to this policy I have won to the federation many great and noble peoples, who under the ancient traditions of the inner world would have been massacred or enslaved after we had conquered them; and thus I won the Luanians. I gave them their freedom, and returned their weapons to them after they had sworn loyalty to me and friendship and peace with Ja, and I made the old fellow, who had had the good sense to surrender, king of Luana, for both the old chief and his only son had died in the battle.

When I sailed away from Luana she was included among the kingdoms of the empire, whose boundaries were thus pushed eastward several hundred miles.

We now returned to Anoroc and thence to the mainland, where I again took up the campaign against the Mahars, marching from one great buried city to another until we had passed far north of Amoz into a country where I had never been. At each city we were victorious, killing or capturing the Sagoths and driving the Mahars further away.

I noticed that they always fled toward the north. The Sagoth prisoners we usually found quite ready to transfer their allegiance to us, for they are little more than brutes, and when they found that we could fill their stomachs and give them plenty of fighting, they were nothing loath to march with us against the next Mahar city and battle with men of their own race.

Thus we proceeded, swinging in a great half-circle north and west and south again until we had come back to the edge of the Lidi Plains north of Thuria. Here we overcame the Mahar city that had ravaged the Land of Awful Shadow for so many ages. When we marched on to Thuria, Goork and his people went mad with joy at the tidings we brought them.

During this long march of conquest we had passed through seven countries, peopled by primitive human tribes who had not yet heard of the federation, and succeeded in joining them all to the empire. It was noticeable that each of these peoples had a Mahar city situated near by, which had drawn upon them for slaves and human food for so many ages that not even in legend had the population any folk-tale which did not in some degree reflect an inherent terror of the reptilians.

In each of these countries I left an officer and warriors to train them in military discipline, and prepare them to receive the arms that I intended furnishing them as rapidly as Perry's arsenal could turn them out, for we felt that it would be a long, long time before we should see the last of the Mahars. That they had flown north but temporarily until we should be gone with our great army and terrifying guns I was positive, and equally sure was I that they would presently return.

The task of ridding Pellucidar of these hideous creatures is one which in all probability will never be entirely completed, for their great cities must abound by the hundreds and thousands in the far-distant lands that no subject of the empire has ever laid eyes upon.

But within the present boundaries of my domain there are now none left that I know of, for I am sure we should have heard indirectly of any great Mahar city that had escaped us, although of course the imperial army has by no means covered the vast area which I now rule.

After leaving Thuria we returned to Sari, where the seat of government is located. Here, upon a vast, fertile plateau, overlooking the great gulf that runs into the continent from the Lural Az, we are building the great city of Sari. Here we are erecting mills and factories. Here we are teaching men and women the rudiments of agriculture. Here Perry has built the first printing-press, and a dozen young Sarians are teaching their fellows to read and write the language of Pellucidar.

We have just laws and only a few of them. Our people are happy because they are always working at something which they enjoy. There is no money, nor is any money value placed upon any commodity. Perry and I were as one in resolving that the root of all evil should not be introduced into Pellucidar while we lived.

A man may exchange that which he produces for something which he desires that another has produced; but he cannot dispose of the thing he thus acquires. In other words, a commodity ceases to have pecuniary value the instant that it passes out of the hands of its producer. All excess reverts to government; and, as this represents the production of the people as a government, government may dispose of it to other peoples in exchange for that which they produce. Thus we are establishing a trade between kingdoms, the profits from which go to the betterment of the people—to building factories for the manufacture of agricultural implements, and machinery for the various trades we are gradually teaching the people.

Already Anoroc and Luana are vying with one another in the excellence of the ships they build. Each has several large shipyards. Anoroc makes gunpowder and mines iron ore, and by means of their ships they carry on a very lucrative trade with Thuria, Sari, and Amoz. The Thurians breed lidi, which, having the strength and intelligence of an elephant, make excellent draft animals.

Around Sari and Amoz the men are domesticating the great striped antelope, the meat of which is most delicious. I am sure that it will not be long before they will have them broken to harness and saddle. The horses of Pellucidar are far too diminutive for such uses, some species of them being little larger than fox-terriers.

Dian and I live in a great palace overlooking the gulf. There is no glass in our windows, for we have no windows, the walls rising but a few feet above the floor-line, the rest of the space being open to the ceilings; but we have a roof to shade us from the perpetual noon-day sun. Perry and I decided to set a style in architecture that would not curse future generations with the white plague, so we have plenty of ventilation. Those of the people who prefer, still inhabit their caves, but many are building houses similar to ours.

At Greenwich we have located a town and an observatory—though there is nothing to observe but the stationary sun directly overhead. Upon the edge of the Land of Awful Shadow is another observatory, from which the time is flashed by wireless to every corner of the empire twenty-four times a day. In addition to the wireless, we have a small telephone system in Sari. Everything is yet in the early stages of development; but with the science of the outer-world twentieth century to draw upon we are making rapid progress, and with all the faults and errors of the outer world to guide us clear of dangers, I think that it will not be long before Pellucidar will become as nearly a Utopia as one may expect to find this side of heaven.

Perry is away just now, laying out a railway-line from Sari to Amoz. There are immense anthracite coal-fields at the head of the gulf not far from Sari, and the railway will tap these. Some of his students are working on a locomotive now. It will be a strange sight to see an iron horse puffing through the primeval jungles of the stone age, while cave bears, saber-toothed tigers, mastodons and the countless other terrible creatures of the past look on from their tangled lairs in wide-eyed astonishment.

We are very happy, Dian and I, and I would not return to the outer world for all the riches of all its princes. I am content here. Even without my imperial powers and honors I should be content, for have I not the greatest of all treasures, the love of a good woman—my wondrous empress, Dian the Beautiful?

A CATALOG OF SELECTED
DOVER BOOKS
IN ALL FIELDS OF INTEREST

A CATALOG OF SELECTED DOVER

BOOKS IN ALL FIELDS OF INTEREST

CONCERNING THE SPIRITUAL IN ART, Wassily Kandinsky. Pioneering work by father of abstract art. Thoughts on color theory, nature of art. Analysis of earlier masters. 12 illustrations. 80pp. of text. 5⅜ x 8½.   23411-8

ANIMALS: 1,419 Copyright-Free Illustrations of Mammals, Birds, Fish, Insects, etc., Jim Harter (ed.). Clear wood engravings present, in extremely lifelike poses, over 1,000 species of animals. One of the most extensive pictorial sourcebooks of its kind. Captions. Index. 284pp. 9 x 12.   23766-4

CELTIC ART: The Methods of Construction, George Bain. Simple geometric techniques for making Celtic interlacements, spirals, Kells-type initials, animals, humans, etc. Over 500 illustrations. 160pp. 9 x 12. (Available in U.S. only.)   22923-8

AN ATLAS OF ANATOMY FOR ARTISTS, Fritz Schider. Most thorough reference work on art anatomy in the world. Hundreds of illustrations, including selections from works by Vesalius, Leonardo, Goya, Ingres, Michelangelo, others. 593 illustrations. 192pp. 7⅛ x 10¼.   20241-0

CELTIC HAND STROKE-BY-STROKE (Irish Half-Uncial from "The Book of Kells"): An Arthur Baker Calligraphy Manual, Arthur Baker. Complete guide to creating each letter of the alphabet in distinctive Celtic manner. Covers hand position, strokes, pens, inks, paper, more. Illustrated. 48pp. 8¼ x 11.   24336-2

EASY ORIGAMI, John Montroll. Charming collection of 32 projects (hat, cup, pelican, piano, swan, many more) specially designed for the novice origami hobbyist. Clearly illustrated easy-to-follow instructions insure that even beginning papercrafters will achieve successful results. 48pp. 8¼ x 11.   27298-2

THE COMPLETE BOOK OF BIRDHOUSE CONSTRUCTION FOR WOOD-WORKERS, Scott D. Campbell. Detailed instructions, illustrations, tables. Also data on bird habitat and instinct patterns. Bibliography. 3 tables. 63 illustrations in 15 figures. 48pp. 5¼ x 8½.   24407-5

BLOOMINGDALE'S ILLUSTRATED 1886 CATALOG: Fashions, Dry Goods and Housewares, Bloomingdale Brothers. Famed merchants' extremely rare catalog depicting about 1,700 products: clothing, housewares, firearms, dry goods, jewelry, more. Invaluable for dating, identifying vintage items. Also, copyright-free graphics for artists, designers. Co-published with Henry Ford Museum & Greenfield Village. 160pp. 8¼ x 11.   25780-0

HISTORIC COSTUME IN PICTURES, Braun & Schneider. Over 1,450 costumed figures in clearly detailed engravings–from dawn of civilization to end of 19th century. Captions. Many folk costumes. 256pp. 8⅜ x 11¾.   23150-X

THE STORY OF THE TITANIC AS TOLD BY ITS SURVIVORS, Jack Winocour (ed.). What it was really like. Panic, despair, shocking inefficiency, and a little heroism. More thrilling than any fictional account. 26 illustrations. 320pp. 5⅜ x 8½.

20610-6

FAIRY AND FOLK TALES OF THE IRISH PEASANTRY, William Butler Yeats (ed.). Treasury of 64 tales from the twilight world of Celtic myth and legend: "The Soul Cages," "The Kildare Pooka," "King O'Toole and his Goose," many more. Introduction and Notes by W. B. Yeats. 352pp. 5⅜ x 8½.   26941-8

BUDDHIST MAHAYANA TEXTS, E. B. Cowell and others (eds.). Superb, accurate translations of basic documents in Mahayana Buddhism, highly important in history of religions. The Buddha-karita of Asvaghosha, Larger Sukhavativyuha, more. 448pp. 5⅜ x 8½.   25552-2

ONE TWO THREE . . . INFINITY: Facts and Speculations of Science, George Gamow. Great physicist's fascinating, readable overview of contemporary science: number theory, relativity, fourth dimension, entropy, genes, atomic structure, much more. 128 illustrations. Index. 352pp. 5⅜ x 8½.   25664-2

EXPERIMENTATION AND MEASUREMENT, W. J. Youden. Introductory manual explains laws of measurement in simple terms and offers tips for achieving accuracy and minimizing errors. Mathematics of measurement, use of instruments, experimenting with machines. 1994 edition. Foreword. Preface. Introduction. Epilogue. Selected Readings. Glossary. Index. Tables and figures. 128pp. 5⅜ x 8½.   40451-X

DALÍ ON MODERN ART: The Cuckolds of Antiquated Modern Art, Salvador Dalí. Influential painter skewers modern art and its practitioners. Outrageous evaluations of Picasso, Cézanne, Turner, more. 15 renderings of paintings discussed. 44 calligraphic decorations by Dalí. 96pp. 5⅜ x 8½. (Available in U.S. only.)   29220-7

ANTIQUE PLAYING CARDS: A Pictorial History, Henry René D'Allemagne. Over 900 elaborate, decorative images from rare playing cards (14th–20th centuries): Bacchus, death, dancing dogs, hunting scenes, royal coats of arms, players cheating, much more. 96pp. 9¼ x 12¼.   29265-7

MAKING FURNITURE MASTERPIECES: 30 Projects with Measured Drawings, Franklin H. Gottshall. Step-by-step instructions, illustrations for constructing handsome, useful pieces, among them a Sheraton desk, Chippendale chair, Spanish desk, Queen Anne table and a William and Mary dressing mirror. 224pp. 8⅛ x 11¼.

29338-6

THE FOSSIL BOOK: A Record of Prehistoric Life, Patricia V. Rich et al. Profusely illustrated definitive guide covers everything from single-celled organisms and dinosaurs to birds and mammals and the interplay between climate and man. Over 1,500 illustrations. 760pp. 7½ x 10⅛.   29371-8

Paperbound unless otherwise indicated. Available at your book dealer, online at **www.doverpublications.com**, or by writing to Dept. GI, Dover Publications, Inc., 31 East 2nd Street, Mineola, NY 11501. For current price information or for free catalogues (please indicate field of interest), write to Dover Publications or log on to **www.doverpublications.com** and see every Dover book in print. Dover publishes more than 500 books each year on science, elementary and advanced mathematics, biology, music, art, literary history, social sciences, and other areas.